TEETONCEY

Other Children's Books by Theodore Taylor:

Theodore Taylor

TEETONCEY

Illustrated by Richard Cuffari

Doubleday & Company, Inc.   Garden City, New York

ISBN: 0-385-09584-8 Trade
0-385-09587-2 Prebound
Library of Congress Catalog Card Number 73–13097
Text copyright © 1974 by Theodore Taylor
Illustrations copyright © 1974 by Richard Cuffari

For

Alma Ruth "Duck" Macrorie

who is now telling St. Peter how to decorate heaven.
With many colors; much laughter.

Laguna Beach, Calif.
March 1973

SHIPWRECK

In the lookout cupola of the red-roofed Heron Head Lifesaving Station, on the Outer Banks of North Carolina, young Mark Jennette, surfman, peered seaward through streams of water on the pane. It was like sighting through a glaze of ice. He could barely see the beach; the raging breakers. Gusting wind shook the building. His watch had begun at noon, and he was relieved that it was nearing an end. No one was out on foot or sand pony patrol because of poor visibility. Only Jennette was watching the sea and it was a useless effort.

Below him, at various places in the two-story shingled building, were the five other Heron Head surfmen, along with the commanding officer, Keeper Filene Midgett. They went about work saying little but fully realizing that before this day and night were over, they might have to crew the six-oared boat and go out through the crashing surf. There was not a man among them who was not deathly afraid of the sea. They knew its might. Yet there was not one, and there never had been, who would refuse to take his seat in the oak-ribbed craft.

On the first floor of the building was the boatroom, the combined mess and crew off-duty room; the Keeper's room and a storeroom. That room contained the breeches buoys, signals and rockets; a life car, tools and other apparatus to save lives. The doors to the boatroom were wide and heavy, opening to a sloping platform so that the boats could be quickly pulled out on to the beach. There was another door on the opposite side in case the boats would have to travel overland.

The second floor contained cots for the men and a space for survivors who were hauled, often more dead than alive, from the ocean. This space had been filled on more than one occasion.

A few minutes before four o'clock, Jabez Tillett, an older man, wound up into the lookout cupola to take the watch. "See anythin', Mark?" he asked, squinting futilely out the window.

"Nothin' but rain. Surf's gone mad."

They exchanged uncertain, worried looks and then Jennette went down the ladder to the mess for a mug of coffee.

Outside, the high flagstaff, used to signal passing ships with international flags, bent from the force of the wind; rain slanted over the low dunes to flatten the few clumps of long grass on inland where a handful of trees dodged frantically, clinging to roots.

During the worst storms the tide sometimes flooded in over the Banks, the chain of narrow, almost barren islands between Currituck Sound, Roanoke Sound, Pamlico Sound, Core Sound and the ocean. The shallow sounds were to east, fresh water tainted with salt, making it brackish; home to fish, crab, oysters, clams and scallops. They were dotted with pound poles for fishing nets. It was mullet and shad country.

The islands stretched like a thin, drawn hunter's bow for a hundred seventy-five miles from up around Knott's Island, near the Virginia border, down to Cape Lookout, cutting sharp west at Hatteras Lighthouse and the vicious Diamond sand bars. Over the years surging seas cut new inlets, and new islands would be born. Then the sea and sand would fill in, closing the inlets.

The few people who lived on the narrow fingers of shifting barrier sand, lapping water on both sides of them, were called Bankers.

At 4:40 the *Malta Empress* grounded with a muffled boom, piling up on a sand bar a quarter mile offshore, breaking her back; snapping two of her masts as if they were twigs. The roar of the shoal water deadened the agony of splintered wood and the pops of severed rigging as she began to come apart.

In the dining saloon, the oil lamps squirted from their gimbals to splatter against the forward bulkhead, one of them sending flames up the wet wood.

The woman and the girl picked themselves up off the deck as the man rushed into the shadows. His face was as gray as the seas outside. Trying to get

his breath, believing they were about to die, he attempted to remain calm. "We've hit the beach. We must go."

His wife nodded, and he clung to them for a moment to murmur, "I love you both." Then he lifted the girl up, folding her into his arms. "Hold tight to me. Keep your eyes closed," he said. He had already seen what was out there.

The girl nodded and pressed her white lips together, clinging to him desperately.

They went up the shaking companion and out on to the deck as water rose in the dining saloon. Seas were beginning to bore across the shattered hull, carrying wreckage, sweeping everything in the path.

They looked ahead. On the bow were a few vague forms, huddling together. Beyond that, in the twilight murk, were towering breakers.

A voice behind them, the captain's, yelled over the din. "Go to the bow! Go to the bow!"

The wife held to the husband's arm for a brief moment but then her feet were sliced away by a length of broken railing; her head was smashed against the deck housing. The girl saw it all and screamed. The mother twisted lifelessly forward in foam and debris; her body entangled in the broken railing.

The next icy sea caught the man and the girl, tossing them over the side. Choking, they hit bottom and then were propelled to the raging surface as the ship disintegrated behind them.

He shouted, "Hang on," and began to kick in what he thought was the direction of the beach.

He fought his way almost to the breaker line, but the first heavy curl ripped them apart and the girl, separated from her father, tumbled over and over, slamming into the bottom headfirst, then rising in the water, stunned, to be trapped under another curl. Spun over, she slammed again to the bottom, her head ramming into compacted sand.

Everything went black.

She had arrived on the Outer Banks, "The Graveyard of the Atlantic," in this year of 1898.

1.

After dark, about six, the driving rain stopped. Then the wind slackened off a bit, dropping its whine. The gale was going inland at last to rake the autumn cornfield stubble on the mainland and then dwindle out against the far-off Blue Ridge peaks.

The brown-eyed boy in faded overalls and a blue shirt, dark hair atangle—Ben O'Neal—stood by the window, looking out through beads of water, seeing nothing, but somehow glad that the storm was over. A gale such as this had taken his father, John, a surfman. A squall in the sound had taken his youngest brother, Guthrie. Of certainty, the O'Neals had already paid their dues to the sea, and it was not likely they would have to pay again.

His oldest brother, Reuben, second mate on the coasting brig *Elnora Langhans,* was somewhere between Carolina and Trinidad, but Ben was sure he was safe. Reuben was a fine sailor.

Rachel, his mother, was at the living room table, behind him, sewing silently in the orange glow of the lamp, deep in her own thoughts. Boo Dog, a mound of gold Labrador, slept peacefully by her feet, a familiar position.

So, aside from the tick of the ship's clock, a precise Seth Thomas, which had been salvaged off a wreck in 1889, it was very quiet in the small house, silvered by sand and wind, nestled in a hammock—high ground in a marshy region—over by the sound side, south and west of Heron Head Lifesaving Station.

But Ben knew that the surf was still pounding in, ten or twelve feet high, slamming against the Banks as if to destroy them. Probably churning Diamond Shoals into a mantrap; making seamen caught anywhere near Hatteras, just to south, wish they were snug in port, sipping beer.

This wild night, Ben was thinking, there likely wasn't a sane man, woman or child on the barrier islands who wouldn't have wagered that a ship would crunch in and die. It was a fair bet in any nor'easter.

They were always out there, schooners or brigantines or barks, edging around Hatteras respectfully or skirting Diamond's long sand fingers, full sails bellied nicely in fair weather; main topsail and foresail reefed in foul, everything else furled away. Steamers plodded by, too; wrecked, too. More of them every year.

Ben often watched the constant parade, wishing he was aboard for the Caribbean or headed north to New York or Boston. Anywhere would have been better than these lonely islands. Anywhere.

And while the storms sent his mother into a

gloom, he didn't really mind them if they didn't last long. In fact, the fury excited him. But his mother never failed to mention, once the wind began calling, that more than four hundred ships had crashed on these sands. She'd always find a way to bring up John O'Neal and Guthrie, sometimes without even mentioning their names. She'd done it earlier this day and he'd groaned. It wasn't that he didn't respect them. He did. Especially his father. But he'd never really known them. He was only two when John O'Neal was lost down at Hatteras; only four when Guthrie, who was then thirteen and money fishing for Old Man Spencer, had been swept overboard in Pamlico Sound. He knew them by photographs and stories. John O'Neal was a legend on the Banks.

But many times Ben had been told by others that if all the sailors and fishermen who'd been drowned here would suddenly come back, dating from Sir Walter Raleigh's ships on, two thousand ghosts would be walking the sands. Some nights, in bed, he thought about the ghosts. Those men walking along the beach, hair all matted and clothes ripped up, staring straight ahead; mouths open and walking, walking. Once, he dreamed of seeing his father and Guthrie. Yet, in daylight, it made no sense.

"Stopped rainin', Ben. Fetch some more wood," Rachel said.

Her voice took his mind off the beach.

The stove, an iron hot-box made in Cincinnati, could chase them out when it glowed cherry-red, devouring wood almost as fast as Ben could get it, even with the damper at short choke.

"Ben," she said again.

He nodded and turned away from the window to sweater-up; get his coat and boots. He was only too happy to leave the room. Aside from dashing to the outhouse twice, he'd had to look at Chicago catalogues and do odd jobs while the frame house, tucked at the end of a short lane in red myrtle, a few live oak and some scrub holly, *yaupon*, trembled in the gale. The wood was at the rear of their five rooms.

He tucked his overall pants into his rubber boot-tops, then went out. Boo Dog bounded forward first, pleased to be released. He never seemed to mind cold or plunging headfirst into the chill sound to retrieve ducks, but cared little for stinging rain.

As Ben rounded the back of the house, a flare hung in the black, turbulent sky for a few seconds and he knew instantly what it meant.

A ship was in trouble.

Yet it was odd that he'd come outside at this exact moment; that his mother had sent him out just in time to see the arc; odd that what he'd thought about earlier had come true. His heart began to pound, as usual.

Very likely, the ship had piled up on the shoals and was helpless. It had happened before almost in the same spot. During some storms, more than one ship had climbed up over the shoals, anywhere along the Banks, to come up and crash right on the beach.

It made rescue easy. On a few, the men had simply jumped ashore.

He waited for another distress rocket to curve up but none came.

Licking his lips, feeling the excitement surging higher, that strange mixture that always churned in his stomach when there was a wreck, he told Boo they should go over. Then he quickly gathered an armful of wood and took it inside, dumping it noisily into the box, at the same time announcing that he'd seen a flare.

Rachel glanced up, frowning. He knew she'd rather ignore it. It wasn't that she didn't have sympathy for the ship or survivors. He thought she simply wanted to wall it off; pretend it wasn't there. Scared silly it might be Reuben and the *Elnora Langhans.* He could not fully understand it but knew she had an abiding hatred for the ocean. She hadn't been down to the beach in years. She seldom even looked out across the wide chopping sound toward the mainland.

"I best go over," he said, looking directly at her, hoping for even slight approval.

She increased the speed of her stitches. "They don't need your help, Ben. Filene can do right well without it."

"I best go," he insisted, realizing it was a mistake to even tell her.

She sighed but didn't answer, withdrawing back into herself. A thin woman but strong and durable, as were most Banks women, her nose was long;

hair gray. She wore steel-rimmed spectacles when sewing or reading the Bible. Her skin was smooth, showing few wrinkles. She always wore a big straw hat when gardening. Sometimes she looked severe but was kindly and neighborly to anyone as long as they didn't ask what Ben's plans were. She was capable of hearty laughter and wry humor when the weather was calm.

In truth, now that he'd finished what school there was on the Banks, she was afraid Ben might go money fishing or worse. Might find someone to take him on as a ship's cabin boy instead of working now and then for Mr. Burrus up in Chicamacomico village, which the U. S. Post Office had dumbly renamed Rodanthe because ignorant mainlanders couldn't spell the former. They were both Indian names.

Actually, if she'd had the funds she would have boarded him over in Manteo so he could go on to high school. That wasn't likely, though he could read like a scholar and did his arithmetic well. He should certainly go on to high school, she believed. But she also thought it might be inevitable that he'd follow Reuben to sea. Ben had inherited a silent, stubborn roughness from John O'Neal. He was now, as she saw it, a plain ruffian. Reuben, who could be tender, often talked about dirt farming. Ben only talked about the sea and a man he never knew— John O'Neal.

"I'm goin', Mama," he said. "You hear?"

She didn't answer, just concentrated on her sewing.

Ben lighted the lantern and went out, Boo Dog following. They went down the lane and began slogging across the wet flats and low dunes toward the beach.

Rachel turned to look at the closed door, his persistence, almost insolence, still in her ears. She sighed deeply. She would have taken Ben and left the Banks long ago except that John and Guthrie were in watery graves nearby. Besides, she owned the land on which they lived, and she wouldn't have known what to do on the mainland; where to live. With Ben's help, she brought in occasional money as a netmaker. Then Reuben sent some home. They had enough. The two years' pension that the government had given her after John capsized was long gone.

She sighed again, wondering how long she'd be able to control the boy. Not very much longer, she thought. The Lord knew she'd tried hard enough to tenderize Ben, she was certain. Even to pretending he was a girl when he was in the cradle and for some time after. That hadn't worked very well.

Rachel inspected the stitching and tried to get her mind off Ben.

2.

The November wind cut at Ben and Boo Dog as they neared the last sand hills, not only hearing the roar of the surf but feeling its power as it shook the earth. Wind caught spray off the breaker curls and sent it inland in a fine shower. Ben's face was wet. Boo's thick coat was dotted with crystals of water. Had the temperature dropped another five degrees ice would have started to skim on the ooze of the sound shore; cake around the foxtails in the marshes.

They mounted the final low dune and Ben could vaguely see the surfmen in a small knot on the beach. One was holding a red Coston flare that plumed off smoke, making an eerie scene against the background of slamming breakers and shimmering mist. It was a scene Ben knew. But seeing it again he wished so much that his father was amongst the men so he could feel some party to it.

Two mules had dragged the boat wagon down from the station and a Banker pony had tugged the equipment cart along. The surfmen had already unloaded the gear. But they hadn't set up for a breeches buoy haul, shooting a line out over the ship with the mortar gun; pull in survivors in the swaying canvas sleeve. Nor had they launched the boat.

Boo Dog began barking at the mules and Ben yelled for him to quiet down. He grabbed his scruff and whacked him good, then looked out to sea, trying to pierce the darkness over the crashing rows of breakers, hoping to spot a mast. There was nothing out there. Or, if there was, it was secreted in the night and towering waves.

Looking down at the surf line, turned to froth and thick with boiling sand, pale crimson in the final glows of the Coston flare, he saw the awful sight of splintered timbers, broken spars with rigging still trailing; all kinds of debris. He had never seen it this bad. It stretched into the shadows on either side of the small group of men. They were now beginning to spread along the beach.

Ben knew what it meant. The ship had died out there before anyone could help her. Launch the double-ended boat or get a line on board her. There was nothing to do but search for bodies and hope that someone might have survived.

The lone man standing by the cart had despair on his face as he lit another Coston, making himself a sentinel. Ben quickly recognized him as Filene Midgett, commander of the Heron station. He was of some kin to Ben, as was almost everyone on the Banks.

The flare caught and began to burn, casting a hellish glow on shining, reddened skin. Filene glanced at Ben with anything but a welcome look.

Vapor came out of his nostrils and mouth, winding away on the wind. Square-faced, heavy-jawed, he was not pretty to look at, even in sunlight.

"Anythin' I can do to help, Cap'n?" Ben asked, fairly anxious. He could hold the flare, for instance.

Filene shook his head and gazed back at sea.

Ben guessed that he was hoping a swimmer might spot his signal and flop toward it. Watching his heavy features, Ben tried to think of what next to say. He knew Filene and the other surfmen weren't too sure about what he planned to do in years hence. They only knew, even though he was John O'Neal's son, that Rachel had raised him as a girl until he was five, actually putting him in dresses and letting his hair grow long. They didn't know how much damage that had done.

Well, it had done a lot. Ben boiled every time he thought about her doing that. It was a monumental disgrace to do it to a surfman's son.

Once, when he was about nine and hanging around Heron Head station, watching them practice rescues, Filene had asked, "Why 'n tarnation you let that woman keep you in a dress so long?"

It wasn't a fair question, Ben thought. He hadn't had much to say about it when he was five. Filene couldn't reckon with that.

That same afternoon they were practicing with the breeches buoy, firing a line from the Lyle mortar gun over the wreck-pole yardarm; then hauling a man to earth in less than four minutes from the time they started rigging. The breeches buoy looked like a pair of oversized canvas pants and hung from the line on a pulley. The survivor would slip down into it and then hang on for dear life as he swayed over the boiling surf.

To show he wasn't a coward, Ben had said, "Cap'n, let me ride it down."

Filene had laughed. "Go ahead, boy."

Jabez Tillett had said, "Cap'n, mebbe it . . ." All he got was a withering look for butting in.

Ben started up the fifty-foot pole, heart in his mouth, climbing the spikes that were set for men. He got halfway up and didn't think he could make it. He looked back toward the sand. It seemed a thousand feet.

He swallowed and said, "Help me, John." Then went on to the top.

They brought him down in a wild ride that left his knees shaking. The back of his legs felt like jelly all the way home.

All Filene had said was, "You mighty slow goin' up that pole, Ben."

But whatever they thought of Ben, he knew the surfmen were kings on the Banks. Pure royalty. The jobs, though dangerous beyond belief, were prized. As much for pride as for money. The seven men at each station fished mullet or shad or made another living during the summer, but the winter and spring were reserved for patrolling the beaches and plucking survivors off wrecks. The Carolina stations were stretched every seven miles up to the Virginia line.

Of course, menfolk on the Banks had always been

wreckers or lifesavers or had gone to sea in the square-riggers or had fished the sounds in sharpies or Creef boats; ocean-fished with haul nets. It was in the marrow and the worst thing any man could say of another was, "I'd like not to have him in a boat with me." And in the twenty years of the Life-saving Service, no Banker, to anyone's knowledge, had ever shown a white feather; had ever given any-one the opportunity to call him a coward. Ben did not intend to be the first.

"When did she hit?" Ben shouted, determined to make Filene talk.

"Dunno."

"I saw her rocket."

"My rocket," Filene corrected sternly, glaring at Ben.

"Then nobody saw her hit?"

Filene nodded, paying more attention to the sea, naturally, than to Ben.

He was a powerful man, a bit over six feet. His age was about fifty. He'd been a surfman for thirty years, a rescuer even before the Lifesaving Service was founded in 1871. Now, he demanded respect and got it. The same was true of all the keepers. But Midgett was the most famous name in the clan of surfmen. There were a dozen or more in the service.

Filene finally spoke, almost in defense of himself, straining his eyes seaward. He did not really want to speak to Ben, especially this night, but felt he had to talk his piece to someone.

"I sent Luther Gaskins on patrol when she quit

rainin' enough to see ten feet ahead."

The beach patrols always went one half the distance to the next station, punched a clock and turned back. Back and forth. About every hour, meeting the patroller from the next station, usually. But when it was blind with rain or snow it didn't do much good to make the walk or edge along on a sand pony. Sometimes the first anyone knew of a wreck was a pitiful cry from a sailor crawling along the beach.

Filene snorted spitefully. "Alriddy there was wood on the beach. Must 'ave been deep in ballast when she hit the bar.

The men called ships, sky, tide, sea, fish and sun "she." They were all female. Unpredictable, the men said. And mainlanders couldn't understand why the Bankers said some other things. "Mommicked" was fouled-up and "berlask" was ruined. The Bankers did not know, either, but were told that people in northern England had talked that way long ago. Some British professor came out and listened and said it was from Devon, wherever that was. The Bankers shrugged.

"Rain hid her from you all day?" Ben asked, careful not to antagonize Filene but still curious.

Filene nodded bleakly and Ben began to feel the Keeper's rage; perhaps his guilt for not having sent a patrol out earlier. The sea had insulted him once again; had spit in his eye. That was not a healthy thing to do to Filene Midgett.

Ben knew Filene hadn't lost many lives when a

ship got this close. He'd gone out in any weather under oars, six men pulling; him steering, no matter the water, to bring them in. Ben had seen the boats go out, climbing the breakers almost straight up, Filene hunched and braced in the stern over the steering oar; damning the sea without ever once cussing. He was a very religious man.

Ben knew he could lay a Lyle gunshot across a ship for a breeches buoy rig in almost total darkness; do it in less than five minutes once his gun was set. He'd been decorated, as had John O'Neal, for saving lives. Both were gold medal men, winners of the highest Lifesaving Service award.

But this ship, Ben was certain, had come apart like a box of spilled matches when it hit the bar in sheeting rain.

3.

A shout carried over the wind and thunder of water.

Then Jabez Tillett, who was as stringy as the wreck pole and had an Adam's apple like a rock in mid-channel, no chin at all, staggered toward them with a sodden limp bundle on his back. He lowered it to the sand near Filene's boots. The man's mouth was open and his lifeless eyes were filled with terror as if he'd seen something he couldn't believe.

Ben glanced again. The body was broken and sand-dredged, almost stripped of clothing. The legs were at crazy angles. He turned his head. He didn't exactly like looking at dead people. He'd only seen three or four in his lifetime. This man would join the others in walking the beach.

Catching his breath, Jabez yelled, "She's a bad one, Cap'n." Then nodding south, he slopped back that way along the licks of foam. The storm-driven tide was setting down-coast.

Ben took another look at Keeper Midgett who was still grimly inspecting the form on the sand and decided to join Jabez, who would be more friendly.

He ran after him, Boo Dog pacing by his heels. In a moment, he spotted the wind-whipped flickers of several steaming lanterns; then the dim shapes of the surfmen strung out along the beach. They were pulling debris from the water, searching for more victims.

Catching up with Jabez, Ben shouted, "Can I help?"

Tillett yelled, "Go south." Then turned down into the surf, wading out toward flotsam.

Ben dashed on past Mark Jennette, a likable man about twenty-five who lived in Chicky village. Lathered with foam up to his waist, Mark was busy tugging at a spar entangled with line and a huge torn sail.

Another hundred feet and Ben spotted something bobbing in the foam. He stopped and eyed it, afraid it might be another body. Looking back north, he saw that the darkness and spray had already hidden Jennette. Then, setting his teeth, holding the lantern high, he forced himself into the water.

Edging through the foam, a lump forming at the hollow of his throat, Ben finally touched the mound of floating cloth and sighed relief. It was only a hump of mattress, straw washing out of a split. He grabbed it and towed it back to the sand slope, the hammering of his heart beginning to subside. He truly wanted to find someone in the water. Yet he didn't. Perhaps he should just sneak home again.

Another sound carried faintly over the boom of the surf and Ben realized it was Boo Dog. The barks were insistent and Ben looked in that direction, down the beach. Boo was barely visible, though only thirty or forty feet away. Ben dropped the mattress and ran toward him.

Closer, Ben saw what all the barking was about. Something was on the sand, two or three yards up from the foam line. A shape, sprawled out. Maybe a body.

He stopped again and looked north, hoping to see Jabez or Mark moving toward him. But there was only darkness and those whirling clouds of spray.

Forcing himself on again, he drew up and then gasped. A human, not debris, was on the sand, three feet away from Boo. Ben took a deep breath and moved closer, staring down. Finally, he could see the body plainly.

He bent over, hardly breathing. It was a girl. About ten or eleven years old, he estimated. Almost his own age of just-turned twelve. Her blue dress had been pushed up around her waist. One arm was tucked beneath her. Her mouth was half open. Face smudged with sand; bruised and beginning to swell. Sand was in her nostrils and eyes. She looked dead in the dim lantern glow.

Ben backed away, swallowing; then collected his wits. He'd never seen a dead girl. "Stay here, Boo," he shouted, and then took off north.

Jennette was still in the water, struggling with the heavy canvas, trying to see if anyone was beneath it, when Ben floundered up to him.

For a second, Ben couldn't speak. His mouth

opened but nothing but an "ah" came out.

"What is it?" Mark shouted.

Ben swallowed. "Girl!"

"Where?"

Ben pointed, and Jennette dropped the spar, splashing back toward the beach, Ben following as fast as his boots would allow him.

In a moment, the surfman was on his hands and knees by the body.

Feeling queasy, Ben watched as Mark felt her pulse, then took his forefingers to pry her eyelids open. "Still livin' I think," Jennette muttered, and then turned her over on her stomach.

Ben kept watching as the surfman placed her thin cheek on the back of her hand, then began pushing the water from her lungs, pressing down on both sides just above her spine. Water gushed from her open mouth and Ben closed his eyes. For a moment, Ben thought he might become sick. He turned away.

Finally, he heard Jennette shout, "Let's git her to the Cap'n."

The surfman stipped off his oilskin coat to wrap her, and then lifted her up into his arms. Ben fell in beside him as they ran up the beach, his head spinning from all that had happened in just a few minutes. Ben found it difficult to even think.

As they neared the Keeper, Mark yelled, "Ben found one still alive."

Filene squinted at them but didn't answer. He just reached to the cart to jerk out a square of tar-

25

paulin. Throwing it to the sand, he knelt down. He did it from long experience, not even bothering to glance at Mark or Ben.

Jennette dropped to his knees to settle the bundle gently to the canvas and the Keeper peeled the oilskin back.

Panting, Ben stepped forward to take another look at her, carefully avoiding the dead man nearby.

Filene murmured, "Teetoncey." He said no other word. In the manner of Banks' speaking, it meant "small." She was small and fragile. "Teetoncey" was right for her, Ben thought.

Mark raised his voice above the surf noise, nodding toward the dead man, "I think that man brung her almost in. She washed on up, Cap'n. She's been on the beach a coupla hours, I'd guess. Cold as ice, she is."

Filene put his nose against the girl's mouth, trying to catch a faint sour breath, and then reached inside the torn blue dress that was plastered against her body. He ripped it, and then jerking his sou'wester off, put his ear against the girl's heart. In the lantern glow, Ben saw that the skin on her chest was like chalk tinted with blue.

Filene's rough face was wrapped in a frown. Looking up at Ben with an almost angry look, he yelled, "You strong enough to carry 'er? Take 'er to the station. Warm 'er up. Git 'er alive. I'll send someone soon's I can."

Heart thudding faster even now, Ben yelled back, "Our house is closer, Cap'n." It was, by more than a mile. Ben felt a different surge. He could be of more help.

Filene shrugged and stood up.

Ben pulled off his woolen coat and slid the oilskin away from the girl, tossing it back to Mark Jennette, who lost no time in returning to search for more survivors.

Ben folded the girl into the warmth of his jacket as Filene lit another flare, jammed it into the pipe upright on the cart, and was off into the darkness. It was the last Ben would see of him that night.

Leaving the lantern, he lifted the "teetoncey" girl into his arms and began to trot toward home. He was not really aware of her weight until much later. At that, she didn't weigh half a sack of potatoes. The thing that was welling up inside him made her feel light as a cornstalk.

He held tightly to her and drove his feet over the mushy sand. He was wishing the Lord would open a peephole and let John O'Neal take a look.

Boo Dog criss-crossed ahead, barking loudly, mystified by the whole thing.

Ben was hoping she'd live. The habit of praying was not normal to him, but he was praying she'd live.

Whoever she was.

4.

Breathing hard, arms aching from the long haul, Ben kicked the door open and stood on the threshold with his burden. His cheeks felt as if they were flaming from the cold and exertion. "Mama, it's a girl," he said. "Half drownded. Mebbe dead."

Rachel sucked in her breath and rose up quickly, dropping her sewing to the table. "Put her on the couch."

Ben went on in and gently lowered the survivor down while his mother bent over, pulling the damp coat away from the girl's head, then opening the rest like an envelope. She lifted a thin, limp wrist and held a finger to it while Ben watched, still breathing hard, studying the blue-white face. The girl sure looked dead.

"Some pulse," Rachel said. "Not much."

She straightened up, making plans, chewing her lower lip, the only nervous habit she had. "Now, let's hurry, Ben. You build the fire up, an' I'll need some hot water. An' pull that small bed o' yours into here . . ."

Like most women on the Banks, she'd usually known what to do in an emergency. She'd done her share of mid-wifing, helping in births. There were no doctors on the sandstrips. Nearest one was Meekins, up in Manteo. In emergencies, the Keepers and the womenfolk were the doctors. Mrs. Fulcher, from Big Kinnakeet village, had amputated her husband's leg after a sting ray had poisoned him. She'd done a nice job of it, Doc Meekins had said.

As Ben began chunking wood into the stove, his mother added, "You keep your back turned. I got to take her dress off, what's left of it, an' clean her up. Lord above, she's eaten a bushel o' sand. Mouth, ears, nose."

Ben ran into the kitchen to fill the kettle from the bucket on the sink drainboard, unable to believe his luck that he'd gone to the beach and that Filene had let him take this survivor. Usually, Filene just blew him out of the water with some choice words.

"Soon's you can, get me some cotton, Ben. I got to make a swab. An' get me one of your flannel night-shirts, too."

Ben nodded and filled the kettle. "Will she live?" he asked, replacing the kettle on the stove in the living room. It was beginning to rumble as the wood flared. They didn't use the kitchen range once it was sundown.

"She may if you hurry an' don't pester me with questions," his mother answered. "Poor thing. Half frozen. Blue as a week-old mackeral. If I wasn't a

31

woman I'd curse that sea all the way back to Noah's Ark." Her hands were busy.

Then Rachel laughed weakly. "Why, she's built like a well-made hairpin."

Ben wanted to take a good look at her, even see her naked, and see what his mother was doing. He was simply curious, and felt some responsibility, too. After all, he'd found her. Yet, if the girl was dying he didn't particularly want to see that.

"Let me know when the water biles."

He went into the bedroom for the nightshirt and heard her call again. "An' bring me one of them big towels, one with rough nap. Outta that Sears box."

He carried them in and then saw that air was coming off the kettle. Pouring some water into a tin pan, he got that to her.

For the next few minutes while she kept making demands, Ben kept backing toward her. She was kneeling by the couch cleaning the girl with a big Florida sponge and warm water. She muttered now and then, talking to herself more than the girl. "Hateful. Tearin' this lil' thing to bits. Stuffin' her full o' sand."

That was all directed at the sea, Ben knew.

Finally, his mother pulled the nightshirt down over the small body and smoothed it. The girl was decent now. Rachel sighed, "That's as much as we can do for her at the moment. We have to resign her to the Lord now." She rose up and carried the girl to Ben's bed, tucking her in.

Ben looked at his mother. Her face was pink from labor; beads of sweat dotted her forehead. At this time, he loved her once again.

Then he walked over to the bed. Only the head was peeking out from beneath the crazy-patch comforters. The face had lost some of its blueness. Although it was a thin face, it might be rather pretty, he saw. There was still some grit in her hair which was the hue of a fresh daisy from the mainland.

Rachel was rubbing the small of her back with her hands. All the kneeling had gotten to her and discomfort had swayzed around to her spine. "Pick up her things, Ben, an' take 'em out to the kitchen. I'll wash 'em in the mornin'."

Ben nodded and went to the couch, picking up the torn wad of dress from the floor, along with a slip. He noticed that there were little blue bows around the collar of the slip. There were also some grimy cotton underpants. He picked those up gingerly, feeling embarrassed. Then he saw a small shoe that was already warping and turning white from salt stain. He hadn't remembered it being on her foot. He looked at it a minute and then went on into the kitchen.

Dumping her things, he glanced into the cracked, mottled mirror over the sink. Somehow, his face looked different, he thought. He had his father's long face and jaw. Also his curly, dark hair. He had his bones. Starved ox-bones, his mother had once said. It was a fool thing to think, yet his face seemed different. Even more like that photograph of his father on the dresser.

When he got back to the living room, he saw that his mother had drawn up a straight chair to the foot of the bed. Her hands were beneath the covers. "I'm rubbin' her feet," she explained. "If your father an' brother had gotten ashore, I'd of rubbed their feet, an' mebbe they'd still be alive. When somebody's dyin', Ben, the touch of a human hand is the best thing. Let 'em know someone cares. They seem to know. Up in their head, they're graspin' out for a helpin' hand."

Ben considered all that, watching meantime.

"Reach under an' take a hand," she said. "Don't let any cold air in but jus' rub it, very softly. You rub hard an' you'll take skin off. She's tender now."

Suddenly, Ben felt ill at ease. He didn't even know this scrawny, swelling girl in his own nightshirt and on his own bed. For all he knew she'd be buried six feet under in another day. Filene would read the services according to the surfman's manual and the Good Book.

He held back.

"Do as I tell you, son."

Reluctantly, he reached under and found a hand. Still feeling strange about it, he began to rub very gently, watching her face. It was total blank, but she did seem to be breathing, ever so slightly. That, he could see.

She had a thin, pointed nose and long dark eyelashes. Her lips were a little puffy so he couldn't tell

34

whether they were narrow or not. In fact, her eyes were getting puffy, too, and she had a nasty bruise on her forehead. Her cheekbone, which was high, was scraped on the left side from the tumbling in the surf. Little dots of blood had dried on it.

"What kind of girl is she?" Ben asked.

Rachel laughed. "Well, I don't rightly know how to answer that question, Ben. She's jus' a lil' thing that the sea give up."

"I mean, Mama, is she American?"

"Who's to know what she is? Mebbe we can ask her when she comes aroun'?"

"An' if she don't?"

There was a silence from the end of the bed. He looked down that way. His mother was staring at him as if he'd said the wrong thing.

"You jus' keep rubbin' that hand an' will some of your strength an' warmth into her. You hear?"

5.

Boo Dog had come over and was snoring by Ben's feet, after having sniffed along the edge of the comforters, pushing his big head up, trying to decide who the stranger was; why she was there; what all the fuss was about.

Outside, there was still some force in the wind. It gusted now and then unexpectedly, as if it wanted to remind everyone that it would be back again; rattling the house to make its point. Sometimes Ben wasn't sure that the wind and the sea weren't alive; could think.

The only other sound was the low seething of the stove, now red hot. Ben couldn't stand the silence. "When'll she come aroun'?"

"When she gets good 'n' ready. Then I'll slip a dose of jalap an' calomel down her."

That would make her stand on end, he thought. That *jalap* powder had to be the most rotten medicine on earth. Reuben had brought it home a long time ago. Mixed with calomel and molasses, it was worse than being sick. Worse than having flu. It brought steady and direct trips to the outhouse.

"Pneumonia's what we got to guard against now," Rachel said.

She knew her herb medicines. *Penetrates,* she called them. The recipes were passed back and forth all over the islands, according to what the ailment was. One was tacked up on the kitchen wall, up from an old lady in Buxton Woods.

White moss from lighthouse graveyard
Polybody wine leaf, green and prettysome
when picked on new moon
Boil to a strength, add milk
Boil to a pint.

It would make a pint of *penetrate,* and surely this girl would have her taste of it, Ben thought.

The hand was beginning to warm a bit although it still felt limp as fresh hog gut. He began to wish she'd do something. Cry or yell. Even shiver.

"I wonder where she came from?" He couldn't help but ask.

After a long while, Rachel answered. "We may know in the mornin'. Long's they pick up enough pieces o' that wreck."

"She looks American."

There was a sigh from the end of the bed. "Ben, slip your hand out neatly. Then go in the kitchen an' pick up that dress. Look at the collar. See if there's a label."

He brought it back out to the living room and held it beneath the lamp glow. The stitching was faded but readable. "Durrant. 116 New Bond Street,

37

London. That's in England!"

Rachel's eyebrows raised. "I declare. There. Now, you know that much."

"She's British," Ben said, with some awe. He couldn't ever remember seeing a British girl, much less touching one.

"Not necessarily. That's where the dress come from. Mebbe she didn't. Mebbe she come from New York or Boston. Those clothes look rich, anyway."

Ben thought about the shoe and went back for it. He brushed sand out of the inside. The word "Knowles" appeared and he repeated it. "Mebbe that's her name?"

Rachel said, "I've never heerd o' people puttin' their names in their own shoes."

He examined the girl again. She did look kind of foreign now, no matter what his mother had said.

Returning to the bed, he rubbed the right hand for a long time and then rubbed the left hand. It didn't seem too odd now. Besides, she wasn't awake to know what he was doing. It was just that he'd never been around girls too much. The Scarboroughs, who lived about an eighth of a mile north, in another hammock, had a daughter named Lucy, but he hadn't had much to do with her. Willy Ann Gillikin was up three houses, a mile away, but he hadn't had much to do with her, either.

Soon, he fell asleep due to the high heat in the room and his mother shook him and told him to go to bed. He took another look at the small white face, got a blanket and sprawled out on the couch, becoming aware he hadn't even taken his sea boots off. He kicked them free and then pulled the blanket up.

He watched the girl until he drifted off, thinking many things; feeling content with himself. He hadn't stopped once to rest on the way from the beach; he'd gone at a trot with her even when his lungs started to knife. He'd saved a life. Well, not exactly. Yet. But . . .

He did not awaken until about two o'clock in the morning when there was a pounding at the door. Rachel left the bedside to answer it. He sat up.

Mark Jennette was in the doorway, looking very tired. His eyes were bloodshot, his red hair mussed up after taking the sou'wester off. His mustache was peppered with dry salt. The surfmen were still out on the beach searching, Ben was certain.

"Girl still alive, Mis' O'Neal?" Mark asked.

"She's still livin'."

"Cap'n said for you to keep 'er that way."

Rachel's back stiffened. It sounded like a threat. "You tell Filene Midgett I'm doin' ever blessed thing I can for her. You tell him to come over here hisself if he can do better."

The red-headed surfman turned meek. "Yessum."

Then he looked past Rachel's shoulder to the form on the bed. Satisfied, he nodded and stepped back to the sand.

"Anybody else live?" Rachel asked.

Ben could barely hear Mark's answer. "No, mam."

As the door closed Ben looked across the room to the blurred white patch in the shadows. Now he knew that the sea had taken everyone except this "teetoncey" girl.

"Go back to sleep, Ben," Rachel said softly.

He watched as she sat down in the chair again. He saw that the Bible was on the bed beside the girl and made a guess that his mother had read it for quite a while before placing it against the girl's shoulder.

He listened as she began to hum a hymn. He also noticed there was a look on her face that he'd never seen before. He thought about it a moment. She'd always wanted a girl. Now, she had one. Even temporarily.

He fell asleep studying her bony face.

About six, when it was still pitch outside, he heard his name being called, quietly but urgently. He got up and padded over.

The girl seemed to be awakening. Her mouth opened and she swallowed. Then her eyes opened weakly and closed. They opened again but didn't focus.

"You're safe, everythin's all right, child," Rachel said, speaking in not much more than a whisper, her fingers lightly stroking the girl's forehead.

Ben held his breath.

The girl shuddered, let out a tiny moan, and then the eyelids went down again and closed tight.

Rachel sighed and shook her head. "When you get that weak, all's you want to do is sleep." She looked away. "Or die."

She got up from the straight chair. "I'll make some coffee an' put your breakfast on."

6.

On the outer islands, the work day was from *can to can't*. "Can see to can't see." Dawn was called "the peep o' day" or "calm daylight."

It wasn't much past that, early sun putting gold edges on the broken eastern storm clouds, when Filene jogged up on his Banks pony, dwarfing it. Though small, the shaggy animals were strong. Eating salt-water grasses, pawing sand to dig a hole for fresh water, taking whatever shelter they could from the storms, the sand ponies, *tackies*, managed to survive in the rugged land.

Supposedly, they came to the Banks in the 1700s when the *Prince of India* wrecked off Ocracoke. Some of her cargo of fine Arabian ponies, perhaps bound for Virginia plantations or up Edenton way, swam ashore along with two handlers. Now there were some rather dark complected people on the Banks named Wahab. Arab became *Wahab*. There was also someone named Pharaoh on that vessel. That became *Farrow*. Over the years, like everything else, the looks of the ponies had changed. Their

41

coats had become thick and long; their hooves had spread to handle the mushy sand. They were ugly but useful.

On the stoop, Ben watched as Filene got off his tackie. He didn't need to drop far. His feet were only six or eight inches above the sand when he was aboard her, always bareback. He never said "right" or "left" to her, just *port* and *starboard*. Somehow she knew a sailor straddled her shag and she obeyed.

He nodded to Ben, then said, "Mornin', Rachel, girl still livin'?"

He looked bone- and muscle-weary. His boots were ringed with dried sand and his oilskins were ripped at the seam near the knees. Stubble was on his chin and cheeks. Summer or winter, his skin was always brick-colored.

"Mornin', Filene. Doin' as well as can be expected for all that maulin' she took. You interested in some coffee? I made some fresh."

The burly Keeper sighed and worked the muscles in his broad shoulders, then banged one boot against the other to knock sand off. "Sure am."

"Come on in," said Rachel. "She's beginning to come out o' it, I think. Woke up jus' before daybreak, fluttered her eyes, shivered a lil' an' then went back to sleep. I don't even think she saw us, do you, Ben?"

Ben shook his head as Cap'n Midgett took his hat off and clumped up; then Ben followed his frame in.

She hadn't moved a fraction, he saw. But now that it was daylight her color seemed much better. The forehead bruise, though, was dusky as a grape.

Filene stood over the bed, peering down and Ben wondered what he was thinking. Maybe that she was the only survivor. If she didn't get well, there'd be none. Maybe he was thinking he could have done something to save them all. But who was to know that?

Sipping his coffee, he didn't speak for almost a minute and then said nothing about the girl. But he looked at her intently the whole time.

"Ship was *Malta Empress*. We fetched some manifest papers out o' the wattah. The way the riggin' looks, pieces what has washed up so far, a bark. Spars an' shreds o' skysails, royals, topgallants all mommicked up . . ." He was speaking very low, still eyeing the girl. "Eleven bodies so far, an' we're keepin' on lookin', Rachel. Crew from the Kinnakeets has joined us . . . people from Chicky, Clarks . . ."

His voice trailed off.

It was always that way, Ben thought. Everyone turned out for a shipwreck. Everyone except women like Rachel O'Neal. The grim look on her face said more than words: It was the same old story. Wreckage and bodies. The sea was a killer.

Filene then went on, almost reverently. "I think a man brung this one in, aimin' to get her past the surf. Might have been her daddy. Dressed smart, he was. Then there is a woman looks a lil' like her." He nodded down. "She was tangled up in some railin' when we found her. Busted like a rag doll. Might have been her mom."

"Breaks my heart," said Rachel, with anguish.

43

Ben listened to it all but kept a silence which was what Banks boys usually did around male elders. Especially around Keepers; especially around Filene.

The Keeper raised his tired eyes. They were marbled with red. "Well, I'll send a cart over sometime this afternoon to pick this one up."

"You'll do no such thing, Filene," Rachel stormed. "Are you a lunatic?"

The big man frowned. "Now, I have to take proper custiddy. Make out my report. Get this one to Doc Meekins or have him come to the station. I have my regulations, Rachel. You know the assistant inspector will come down. Always does, when there's a loss o' life . . ."

"Are you plumb out o' your mind, Filene? This child's in shock. She's beggin' for pneumonia. You take her out in that cold air, you may lose her. Besides, you men at that station can't take care o' a girl. Who's to dress an' undress her? Carry her to the outhouse?"

Rachel was wild. Her eyes were full of fire. The skinny body was ready to do battle.

Ben watched in amazement as the Keeper shifted on one foot and then another; rubbed his neck; raked the back of his hand with his whiskered chin. Why was it that the lifesavers could settle a man with a look yet backed away from spindly females?

"I hadn't rightly thought about that, Rachel. I best leave her with you. We'll wait a day or two."

"Or a week or two. Or a month," Rachel replied heatedly.

"All right. All right." His flat of palms came up in defense. "I'll go back to the beach. I'm obliged, Rachel."

He turned slightly. "I'm also obliged to you, Ben."

Ben felt the color rising from his throat into his cheeks. They were the first really decent words Filene Midgett had ever spoken to him.

He nodded.

The Keeper went outside and swung a leg over the pony. He headed through the twisted live oak and myrtle to take the trail that led to the beach, his feet dangling; back stiff as a plank.

Ben glanced over at the girl. She was still motionless.

At about eight o'clock, Ben fed Fid, their own brown and dirty-white tackie, who usually roamed free but had come to the lean-to shelter for the storm. Then he decided to go to the beach. The girl was no more awake than she had been at midnight and he was restless. He had in mind trying to find the other shoe. Mostly, he wanted to see what else had washed up.

From the stoop, Rachel watched him go. He walked with a slight roll, swinging his shoulders easily. So often, the walk reminded her of Ben's father.

She looked across the expanse of island wastes, north and south, taking deep breaths of the cold morning air to cut away the night's weariness. She glanced again at the retreating figure of her son, plodding steadily toward the beach.

It was in the blood, she knew. There was something mystical about these harsh islands and that sea out there that got deep into the muscle and brain of Banks' men. It crept in when they were boys and except for rare occasion stayed like an incurable disease.

They'd sit around and swap the same old stories, telling and retelling the wrecks and rescues. Or talking wind and tide and fish and boats. Likely, Ben would do it, too.

She knew all the stories. She knew what was legend and outright lie and what was truth. For instance, it was a dedicated lie that the Bankers lured ships ashore to steal cargoes, strip the hulls and murder the crews. Far back, most of the families had washed up from wrecks, and it would be the last thing on anybody's mind to cause a ship to ground. An unthinkable thing.

That treacherous story began a hundred or more years ago when it was claimed that land pirates walked ponies, with ship's running lights tied to their necks, along Jockey Ridge, to north, which was the highest sand dune on the Atlantic coast. It was claimed that if a ship was going south, the pony light would be green; north, the light would be red. The ponies made the lights bob, so the ship at sea would figure another ship was in closer and running safe. She'd haul over and pile up on the beach.

It was a terrible lie, Rachel knew.

Even though there was a place below Jockey Ridge named Nag's Head, which supposedly got its title from the lantern-toting ponies, not a word of truth was in that land pirate story. The men would double over in laughter when they heard it. Anyone in their right mind who wanted to lure a ship ashore would put the pony on the beach, not inland on Jock Ridge.

The only time there was murder and some theft was long ago with a Spanish ship. But the vessel wasn't called ashore and the Spaniards had asked for it. They got butchered for their impudence.

There was also the *Flambeau* that wrecked off Chicamacomico, which everyone called Chicky, in 1861. It carried a cargo of top hats. Now, who wouldn't steal a top hat, especially if it threatened to float away? Anyhow, everyone on the Banks had a top hat from the *Flambeau*. Even John O'Neal had one, Rachel remembered, and by no means was he a thief.

Now and then, there was a little purloining of wrecked cargo when whiskey was involved. Some of it mysteriously just never reached *vendue*, which was what the wreck auction was called. But, laughed the Bankers, and Rachel agreed, if everyone in the United States had done no worse than steal top hats and some whiskey, moderately, the country was in good shape.

The people, like Rachel and Ben, were mostly Methodist and God-fearing. In their veins, one family to another, was some British, some Swedish; Irish, Portuguese, German, not to mention Arab. Most of it, to be certain, was castaway blood.

Until he died, Mr. Joshua Dailey was school-master down at Hatteras village and Trent. He had floundered ashore in 1837. In the bad winter of 1856, when the sounds froze up, Mr. Herbert Oden had come bobbing ashore in a pork barrel off the *Mary Varney*, as naked as the moment he was born. Ben's own paternal grandfather, Captain Issac O'Neal, from Plymouth, England, had floated in on a spar, clutching his drowned first mate by the hair of his head.

Rachel knew it all because she'd been born down near Hatteras, daughter of another castaway.

The first people that came to the Banks, after the Indians were pushed out, planned to run cattle and did so for a while. There were still some wild cattle and half-wild sheep around. Soon, though, it was more profitable to be wreckers. In fact, more than a hundred years ago a wreck commissioner was established just to supervise all the hulls that crashed. But the menfolk, just to survive, had to be a little of everything from farmer to boat builder, fisherman and hunter. The women did the rest. As a bride, Rachel had washed, carded and spun her own wool.

True, also, was that many of the houses were built completely of ship's timbers and lumber from the sea; furniture from ship's cabins. If a cargo of red paint washed ashore, houses would be red for years; if puncheons of Jamaica molasses came in, there'd be sweetening for corncakes for a long time to come.

The sea giveth and the sea taketh away, as John and Guthrie were good examples, Rachel thought.

The Outer Banks hadn't been much to look at in the last fifty years, especially since the damn Yankees cut down most of the trees on the sound side in the Civil War. The blowing sand threatened to shove everybody into the sounds if the tide did not accomplish it first. On more than one night, Rachel and Ben had listened to sea water gushing under the house; gotten up in the morning to find the high-ground garden ruined. Only collards could stand that water.

It was certainly no place to raise crops, although across the sounds on the mainland the earth was black and fertile. Corn grew seven feet high over there and Rachel often thought about what life might have been had she been born thirty miles west.

There were still some wide-bladed windmills around to grind grain brought over from the mainland, traded for fish. But most were falling in disuse. People were buying meal instead. She even thought the Banks were showing signs of becoming modern. Telephone lines were hooked between all the lifesaving stations. Telegrams could be sent. The Atlantic & North Carolina railway ran to Morehead City; Norfolk & Southern into Elizabeth City. Steamships of the Old Dominion Line plied the sounds, whistling hoarsely. There was actually a gas engine banged off in the sounds the year before. Perhaps some day the men would do more than fish or make rescues.

And there was a rugged beauty to the Banks that

she acknowledged, one that Ben didn't appear to see. On calm days, there was a quiet over the flats and dunes; over the ridges on down toward Buxton; a feeling of great peace and contentment.

Although mainlanders laughed at it, there was some scraggly vegetation from around Kill Devil Hills and Kitty Hawk on down to Ocracoke Island. Real thick woods around Buxton's high ground. There was gnarled big holly and the scrubbier yaupon with scarlet berries; deerberry, wax myrtle, cedar and dogwood, loblolly pine. Wild flowers grew in some places; wild coffee fern and wild rose. Long grass waved in the silent marshes and ponds, interrupted by foxtails, spike rushes and mincing heron. Roanoke Island, over in the sounds, was bestowed with much green; muskenong grapes big as walnuts.

Because the Gulf Stream ran so close, hitting head-on with the Labrador Current off Hatteras point, there was even the miracle of palmetto and yucca, a few orange trees on south; hibiscus, too. Spanish moss hung in the limbs as it did in South Carolina and Florida.

Here and there were squirrel, rabbit, raccoon and whitetail deer. There was an abundance of gulls and fish hawks; canvasback ducks, redheads, buffleheads; even Canadian and snow geese.

If only the sea was gentler and there were no wrecks.

Rachel looked east, wondering what was happening down on the beach. Ben had disappeared over the dunes.

51

7.

The sun was out strong now and the day was sparkling. The wind had died to a mere steady breeze, setting around to its usual prevail, west of south.

As Ben walked along, he thought about Reuben but firmly believed his brother was still down in the Caribbean, safe enough from any gale blowing up here. He didn't come ashore very often, but when he did Ben would try to make him talk about how it was out there. He didn't talk very much at that and for some odd reason always wanted to work in the garden patch when he got home, if it was spring or summer. Ben couldn't understand it, but Reuben would contentedly hoe and sift the sandy loam in his fingers; even put some in his mouth.

The story of his that Ben liked best was the one of his first trip, when he was still a boy of thirteen. On a bark out of Norfolk. They ran into a storm four days from last landfall at Cape Henry, and Reuben was so sick he thought his belly button would come up.

They ordered him aloft to help furl the top-gallant sail, which was more than midway up the mast, beneath the skysails and royals. It was night, raining, and the big square-rigger was heeling over. He went up the forerigging and got to the foretop. He was so green he didn't know how to get around the running rigging but finally made it to the top-gallant yard.

Two old sailors were already up there and ordered him to go out on the yardarm, but he was too scared to go and hugged the mast. One threatened to knock him off, saying an awful cuss word. It was sixty feet to the deck. Reuben wouldn't budge, though they gestured to kill him, but did go up a second time that night, not knowing anything about what he was doing. Ben admired him greatly.

Yet Reuben would say, "You stay with your mama. That's not a good life out there, Ben."

Well, was there anything good about the Banks for a boy of twelve, finished school? Why couldn't they all realize what he wanted to do was go to sea, then come back sometime and be a surfman? A Keeper, someday. Confession was good for the soul. Yes, be like John O'Neal.

He'd even named his boat *Me and the John O'Neal*. He'd found it in the spring, half-sunk, floating down the cut by Gull Island, over in the sound. He'd waded out to his waist to bring it in. It was a small shad boat, homemade, stoved in on the portside. Not the eighteen or twenty-six footers, with a foresail added to a sprit mainsail and jib, that the Creef and Dough families built up at Roanoke Island. But it looked almost like them, with a round bottom, square stern and sharp prow.

She didn't have a name or number. So he'd claimed it. He painted her new name on the transom after replanking the portside.

Shaving a timber for a mast, he finally got his hands on some old sails and recut them. All summer he'd sneaked off to teach himself to sail. He knew hod would have been raised if his mother had found out about it, but she didn't know a solitary thing about *Me and the John O'Neal*. Or so he thought.

As Ben mounted the last rise the sea opened up before him, tossing rays of sun back into the sky, flinging up glitter from the troughs. The breakers were still high, and the inshore water was murky with sand, but the ocean was flattening out and by afternoon would be blue and peaceful again.

He stopped and let his eyes sweep the horizon. No sails were out there, not even a plume from a steamer. But the ships that had ducked into Hampton Roads, up at Norfolk, would be weighing anchor and pressing on south by sundown. It would be back to normal.

But it just didn't seem possible that this was the same water of last night; that it could go devilish crazy in a few hours; smash ships like toys. Then become gentle and almost smile toward land. But he'd noticed, from time to time, as he'd run along the edge of the surf, that the waves sometimes tried to reach for him. Or maybe he was just imagining it.

He looked out across Heron Shoal. Water was

tumbling over the bar, as it always did. But there was no sign of a ship's grave out there. Not even a piece of broken stick to say that the *Malta Empress* had joined the ghost fleet there the day before.

It wasn't always that way. Sometimes the ships grounded in moderate weather when some mate went to sleep. Before it turned heavy again, the men would go out in boats to take off sugar or salt; molasses or turpentine or coffee. He had once seen them float hundreds of barrels of molasses ashore. Then again, there were those like the *Empress* that sank without a trace except for pieces that hit the shore. Or for survivors like the one now in his own house.

He wondered about her for a moment; if she was indeed British; wondered if she'd come around? He didn't like to think about his mother having to tell her that her parents, if that's who they were, had been claimed and had gone leeward, which was the Banks term for death. "Loo'ard" it was pronounced.

He looked far south. The wreckage had bobbed that way during the night on the surging tide, and, as always, people were on the beach sorting through the debris; helping the surfmen. He could see several wagons and mules; some ponies and carts.

He went in that direction along the littered, storm-gullied sands, Boo Dog winding ahead; sniffing at dead fish and old, feeble gulls that had fought the gale; giving up to flutter down and go loo'ard.

It took about thirty minutes to make the walk and on arriving he saw the usual forlorn piles of jagged wood and tangled, frayed line; ripped sails; parts of hatches and coamings; mattresses; trunks; jugs. Anything that might float or wash.

Nobody was saying much. They never did. They went quietly about gathering the flotsam, as if they were all workers at a funeral. He was hoping to hear someone say, "Heerd you toted 'er home last night, Ben." By now, everyone knew there was a survivor because news on the Banks, word of mouth only, traveled like fire up a powder train. However, Filene had probably already told them everything. There wasn't much else to say.

He did feel better, though, when Mark Jennette came up to ask, "How's she farin'?"

Ben thought it best to quote his mother: "She's holdin' her own."

He went over to where the wet, stained clothing was piled up, not far from canvas humps that covered those not so lucky as the "teetoncey" girl. Although he felt squeamish about it, he took a stick and began turning coats and pants over. He couldn't find a small shoe although there were larger ones and boots.

Filene, who was perched on the Heron station cart, having a pipe, shouted over, "You run to the station, Ben, when that girl can talk. Mebbe she can identify some bodies?" His tobacco smoke was rich and strong.

Ben yelled back that he would and called for Boo. They went north along the beach.

About two o'clock, the girl stirred and came out of it slowly as if groping through wool, opening her eyes to the ceiling of old narrow boards that were bubbled with cracked paint. Some smoke stain was up there, too. She just stared up.

Ben looked up, too, wondering why she was doing it.

Then she frowned and swallowed, licking her lips. They were dry and chapped.

"How do you feel, child?" Rachel asked.

The girl stared at Mrs. O'Neal for a long time. She tried to take a deep breath, but that seemed to hurt down along her ribs. She winced.

"You're safe, child. You're on dry land," Rachel said. Then added to Ben, "She still don't know where she is. Who we are."

The girl slipped back under with a sigh, almost as if she didn't want to know who they were.

"I'll put some yeopon on," said Rachel. It was holly leaf tea.

Mostly, they drank yaupon—which they pronounced "yeopon"—tea because they couldn't afford the other. There were a lot of yaupon bushes scattered about the Banks. The tea men used twigging knives to chop it up, then dried it out between hot rocks in a hollow cypress log. Mainlanders sometimes laughed at the Bankers drinking "holly" tea. But it was never very wise to laugh at a Banker no matter what he was drinking. Bankers would not stand for foolishness or insults.

Ben went out to the kitchen to wash his face and comb his tangled hair. Then he changed his shirt and put on knickers and galluses.

Rachel watched with some interest but said nothing about the preparations. She had an idea that Ben wanted to look good the next time the girl came around. To mention it, though, would cause an explosion. She did smile before turning away. Maybe Ben wasn't quite the ruffian after all. But for several years she'd had some advice to give to mothers on the Banks. Never try to raise a male as a female. They'd go the opposite way, sure as sundown.

Finally, at about four o'clock, Rachel said to the girl, "You jus' can't keep doin' this. I want you to help us get some broth down you . . . I want you to speak to us . . . come back from wherever you are . . ."

That seemed to wake her up more. Ben saw the chapped lips move but nothing came out.

Rachel bent over her; then drew back, looking down. "You're safe on shore, child. You're in North Carolina. In a house. The gale's over."

The girl simply stared as if it made no sense to her.

"I'm Rachel O'Neal an' this is my son, Ben . . ."

Ben nodded and let her see his smile.

She didn't react.

"Now, you try an' stay awake a few minutes. I've had some broth heatin' for you for two hours."

The girl's eyes began to move around the room and Ben followed them.

She looked at the deer head on the opposite wall; at the double-barrel breech loader beneath them. Reuben had shot that buck over at Mattamuskeet.

She looked at everything. The table off the wreck of the *Hermes;* the chest, with brass trimmings, off the *Minna Goodwin.*

Rachel came back with a bowl of broth and a teaspoon. "Let's try an' sit up an' sip a lil' broth," she said.

Ben held the bowl while his mother raised the girl and got her hands out from under the covers. "All right, now, let's open your mouth an' try to sip."

Some went down and she choked.

Rachel said, "Help me, child."

The girl swallowed and some more went down. It took five minutes to get ten spoonfuls down her. Then Rachel said, "She's tuckered out," and let the blond head go back to the pillow. She was asleep again within a minute.

It was after dark when she awakened the next time and they didn't know how long she'd been awake. They were eating supper when they heard the moan. It was almost a hurt animal cry.

Rachel rose swiftly and carried the lamp to the bed. Ben went over, too.

"You were in a shipwreck yestiddy durin' a terrible storm. You remember? You almost drownded. An' Ben here brought you home last night."

Ben nodded.

The girl just looked at them.

"That's why you feel so poorly. But don't fret about it. Jus' lie there an' rest. Get your strength back. We'll tell you everythin' later."

The girl seemed to be making an effort to think. At least, she was staring at them and her eyes narrowed.

Rachel smiled down. "Child, what's your name?"

She opened her mouth, but nothing came out.

Ben could see the confusion grow in panic. She raised up in bed and then fell back. Her chin began to quiver and then tears leaked out of the corners of her eyes. She was too weak to do more than cry silently.

Rachel sat at the edge of the bed and gathered the girl into her arms. She murmured, "That's what I was hopin' for."

"She can't remember her own name?" Ben whispered.

Rachel shook her head violently.

In a few minutes, the girl went back to sleep and Rachel stood up thoughtfully, making some decisions. Finally, she turned to Ben.

"Run over to the station an' tell Filene she's come aroun'. Tell him to get a message to Doc Meekins if the phone line is still up. Have Doc come when he can. But you tell Filene we don't need no visitors tonight, especially him. An' if he asks you what the child's name is, tell him she don't know or can't talk, either one, an' not to bother his head about it."

Ben went to Heron station under a sky chocked with stars, finding it hard to believe that anyone could forget their own name.

He located Filene in the Keeper's room, working on his report of the *Empress* by lantern light. The

60

Keeper always wore his spectacles halfway down the bridge of his nose, and looked out over the top of them. His knotty, meaty hands made the pen a thistle. His hair was the gray of new-forged iron and shocked up. His eyes seemed to be under moss cliffs. Ben was always frightened of him and felt that he somehow never said the right thing.

"She's come aroun'," Ben said.

Filene got up excitedly.

"But Mama said for you to stay right where you are."

The Keeper let out a bellow. "That Mama o' yours ought to have her tongue burnt out."

"She said to get a message to Doc Meekins. Have him come when he can."

"What's that girl's name? I got to write it down."

"She don't know, an' Mama said for you not to bother your head about it."

Filene knocked the chair away from the desk, and Ben scurried off.

8.

Why, he could not exactly say, but the next day Ben tried to stay away from home as much as possible. Maybe it was because they had a stranger in the house, especially the female variety. Maybe it was because the excitement of the wreck was over. He didn't know.

After he'd asked her how she felt in the early morning, he didn't have anything else to inquire about because there was no answer. She'd just stared. Then he caught her looking at him when his back was turned. It made him nervous.

Perhaps it was because the girl looked so funny with those circled eyes and dead-white skin. Besides, he truthfully didn't know what to say to her. How do you talk to anyone who doesn't talk back? Who doesn't have a name? It was like trying to talk to a scared rabbit.

Maybe she was crazy, Ben thought. They could have been bringing her up from somewhere to put her in an insane asylum. They had one in Raleigh, he'd heard.

Ben worked a couple hours for Mr. Burrus out behind the store in Chicky, cleaning hen pens, and then filled a sugar barrel with ducks, head down. They'd go on to Elizabeth City to be iced-up; then to Norfolk.

After that, he took Fid, the tackie, and went up to Big Kinnakeet village for no reason at all and then wound up at Heron Head to talk to Mark Jennette and Jabez about the wreck.

It was Friday, always a dull day at the station. The crew practiced first aid and resuscitation that day; then did routine things. Ben knew the schedule by heart. Monday it was drill with the beach apparatus and overhauling the boats; Tuesday, drill with the boats in the surf; Wednesday, practice with the International flag code signals; Thursday, drills with the wreck pole; Friday, practice pushing water out of victim's lungs. Saturday, housekeeping.

Tuesdays and Thursdays were the best days. Saturday was awful and Ben never went to Heron station on Saturdays. Filene was worse than a fussbudgety woman. He had the men rake the sand even though there wasn't a leaf to fall. The decks were clean enough to roll bread dough on. He refused to call them floors.

Ben waved at Luther Gaskins up in the lookout. On clear days the men on watch peered at passing ships with the long glass, logging them down as to time of passage and direction.

Then he found Jabez and Mark in the equipment room. They didn't seem to be doing much, except keeping out of Filene's way. Jabez asked about the girl.

"Hasn't said a word," Ben replied.

Mark shook his head in dismay. "Hmh."

"I think she's crazy," Ben said.

"Mebbe she's plumb scared to death. She took a beatin' in that surf," Jabez said.

"If that had been a boy, I think he'd of swum on in; kept his head off the bottom," Ben said.

Jabez answered, "I'm not sure o' that, Ben. Wattah that rough, hard for anybody to swim. I got knocked ovah when the *Peggy Neylan* broke up. If it hadn't been for your papa, I'd of never made it. He took a boat hook an' gaffed me like a shirk. Put a hole in me, he did. But better that hole than bein' e't by the shirks an' crabs. I think she done right well. That toide was settin' south somethin' fierce." Jabez always pronounced tide as "toide."

Ben had often heard the story of Jabez getting knocked overboard when the *Peggy Neylan* grounded, and it changed a little each time. This was the first time he'd heard that John O'Neal actually put a hole in Jabez Tillett.

"Well, anyway, I'd a sight rather have had a boy wash up," Ben said.

Mark laughed. "Put six years on you, an' you'd rather have a woman wash up. One 'bout eighteen, with good legs."

They all laughed.

Ben stayed away until almost dark and when he got home there she was, still in bed, staring out from

64

eyes that were pouchy and nearly black around the sockets. He'd never seen a girl with black eyes. They'd turned from the circles to berry color during the day.

Ben gave her a slight wave and went on into the kitchen. "How is she?"

"I think she's better."

"Her eyes blacked up."

"If someone hit you acrost the head with a postie, so would yours."

"She wasn't hit with a postie."

"That sand's just as hard as post wood at the surf line. Where you been all day?"

"Up at the store."

Late next morning, Doc Meekins and the British consul, who wore a derby hat and had what looked like muskrat fur on his coat collar, paid a visit, along with Filene Midgett and the district assistant inspector from the Lifesaving Service, an important man named Timmons. The consul, down from Norfolk, didn't appear to be very happy and walked over the sand like it was swamp mud.

Ben listened to him for a minute. It was certainly strange talk. The consul looked all around, outhouse to Fid's lean-to, and said, "Ext-traaaaaaaward-e-nary."

They'd all boated in, and the sounds can be chilly in November. The consul's oval face was pink from wind and his nose kept dripping. But there was no other way to get to the Outer Banks. Only by boat.

Filene had collected them all at the Chicky dock. Jabez Tillett was minding Filene's cart for the doctor.

Ben stayed outside near Jabez while Meekins checked the girl over in his mother's presence. They never let Meekins tend a female unless another one was present. The women said Doc had "evil hands."

Leaning against the station's wagon, the men talked about the wreck of the *Malta Empress*, but they didn't say anything, in Ben's hearing, that wasn't already known. The consul said he was trying to find out her last port o' call; get a passenger and crew list, if one existed. He said he'd notified, by mail, Lloyd's of London.

Ben whispered to Jabez, "What's that?"

"Insurance people."

About thirty minutes later Doc Meekins came out to say, "Girl has had brain damage, I'm reasonably sure. She may be sufferin' from catatonia or worse." He was a stubby man with muttonchop sideburns and usually smelled of whiskey. He reminded Ben of a hairy peg. He'd doctored Ben once for a broken ankle.

"Catta-what?" Filene asked.

"She may be catatonic. It's another word for confusion and worse. I don't know much about psychiatry. I'm not a brain man, either."

"What causes it?" Filene asked, very much alarmed; shaking his head, his mossy brow furrowed.

Ben had never heard of it, either. But it sounded bad.

"Shock of one kind or another. It can be temporary or permanent. If she has brain damage, fare the' well. She'll be a vegetable. Better you ought to have left her in the surf, Filene."

A vegetable? Ben couldn't believe it. But despite the fact that no one liked him very much, Meekins always seemed to know what he was talking about. He'd gone to school in the North. A place called Harvard.

"How do you cure it?" Inspector Timmons asked.

Doc Meekins rammed some snuff in under his lower lip and sniffed what was left on his stained finger. "You don't. She'll have to, if she can."

Ben wondered how she'd do it.

They all went inside and began to ask questions. Mostly, it was the British consul. *What was her name? When did she come aboard?*

Meekins said, "You're wasting your time."

Where did she live? What was the last port of the Malta Empress?

Ben hung back by the door.

Although the girl seemed much better this day, except for the purple traces beneath the eyes, he could tell she was frightened with so many people around. The consul, who was dressed fancy enough to go to a wedding, was beside himself because she couldn't answer.

Finally, Rachel walked up from the back of the room. "Now, jus' stop, all of you. That's enough."

They quit pestering her and went back outside.

Ben listened again as they talked about what to do

with her. It almost sounded like she was a piece of wreckage that no one would bid on at *vendue*. Jabez looked disgusted and spit a big cud of Ashes' Best Black. That was sweet plug from Statesville. Reuben chewed it, too.

The British consul said he'd have to wait for instructions from the embassy because no one clearly knew if she was British, American or what she was.

Mr. Timmons said he could probably make arrangements to put her in a charity home in Norfolk temporarily.

Doc Meekins said she could probably travel in another week, whether she spoke or not.

Filene didn't say much of anything in the presence of Inspector Timmons now that it had reached this point.

Rachel had come out and had listened for a few minutes. She fumed at them from the stoop. "Never in my life have I heerd grown men talk in such circles. She'll stay right here until she knows who she is."

Doc Meekins cleared his throat as if that circumstance might take a long time. They all looked over at Rachel.

Only Filene was brave enough to answer. "Now, Rachel, don't go aggravatin' this. We all have our official reports to make out . . ."

He got a glare back for his efforts. "Well, you go right ahead an' make 'em out. Meantime, leave her be. *Leave her be!* Filene, I'll never get over you comin' down here yestiddy with those two dead bodies for her to identify . . ."

"Calm down, Rachel," was Filene's embarrassed reply.

Mr. Timmons broke in. "I think we should accept Mrs. O'Neal's kind offer."

The British consul seemed relieved.

So the girl stayed on at the O'Neal house.

They all left, Jabez Tillett driving Doc Meekins in the station cart to his other calls down island. The doctor never came over for just one call. Somebody always had a rupture or the red sprangles—fevers and rashes of one kind or another.

Still outside the house, watching them go, Ben said to his mother, "You hear what Doc said? She may be crazy. He used a word for it. Her brain's hurt."

"He told me 'fore he told them. We'll try to cure her, Ben. Her body's all right. Nothin' was broken."

"He said she might be a vegetable. I've never heard a human called a vegetable."

Rachel took a deep breath. "Ben, she can't talk jus' now. I'm sure she can think, in a matter o' speakin'. She knows when she's bein' talked to. I've noticed that. We have to work with her."

"How?"

Rachel's laugh was hollow. "I don't know. But I do know this. If it was a hurt animal, we'd try to help. Boo Dog don't speak, but if he hurts hisself we try

71

to help. Same with her. And more."

Ben shrugged. If she was loony, an asylum would be the best place for her.

They went inside. She was staring up at the ceiling.

Soon, the girl got her name.

It was at the end of dinner—the first square meal she'd had—*squeteague*, which was gray sea trout, fried, and a boiled potato, milk on the side.

Rachel was trying to be natural. "We do have to call you somethin'," she said, without making too much of it. "Is there any name you want to be called?"

The girl just sat, head down.

They waited. There was no answer.

"Ben?"

He didn't know what to call her. Then he thought of what Filene had said on the beach. It was as good a name as any for now. "Teetoncey."

"That's no name for a girl," his mother protested.

"It's a Banks name."

Rachel laughed, shaking her head. "Well, if that's what you'd like to call her . . ."

Tee became her name.

After dinner, and after she'd had her sponge bath in the tin tub, Ben ordered to sit outside during it, Rachel said, "While I clean the dishes, I want you to talk to her. Jus' talk natural."

"About what?"

Why talk when she wouldn't answer? Why talk

when they didn't even know she could hear? Her brains were mommicked and that was it.

"I don't want to talk to her."

"Ben, I'm not askin', I'm tellin' you."

He felt the fool but sat down on the end of the bed and told her about the lighthouses, the whalebone fences at some of the houses at Kinnakeet and Chicky; the snow geese that came to winter on Pea Island; how the Hatterask Indians had been the first to live here, the Poteskeets up at Kitty Hawk; how the pirate Blackbeard had been cutlassed by Cap'n Maynard not thirty miles from their dock; how the damn Yankees iron-clad *Monitor* foundered off Hatteras.

However, he didn't mention the wrecks and the ghosts that walked the beach at night figuring that might disarrange her more than she was already.

Although she did look at him several times, it was all useless.

He went into the kitchen. "I might as well have talked to a log."

He was disgusted.

9.

Teetoncey *was* built like a well-made hairpin.

Rachel whipped up a nightgown of cotton cloth for her and Saturday morning Tee opened the front door when the sun was far to east, just to look out. It was the first time she'd done that. Ben and his mother watched, wondering what she had in mind. It almost seemed she was afraid to look out.

She was framed a minute in the strong light and Ben could see she had very little meat on her.

Rachel said, absently, "We'll fatten her up, if nothing else." That could be accomplished with hominy grits and juice from slab bacon.

Tee closed the door and went past them into Ben's room and slipped into bed. It had been moved back there.

Ben said, "Think I'll go on up to the store."

Rachel was looking toward the small bedroom. She could see the girl staring out the window. "You know there's nothin' for you to do 'til next week."

That was true, unfortunately.

Rachel said, "See if she'll take to Fid."

Ben sighed and went out to find the sand pony. He was about a quarter-mile away, down near the sound, eating long grass. Ben threw a leg over, grabbed his mane, and said, with irritation, "Let's go to the house."

Fid was more interested in eating and Ben jerked one of his ears to get his attention, and then kicked him in the ribs. The pony wheeled around and began trotting home.

Ben had noticed that Tee had taken to Boo Dog, and he had taken to her. He was on the floor around that bed most of the time now. But there was no secret to that. You rub a dog off and on all day, he'll take to you. Pony might be the same.

Rachel had opened the window and had a handful of corn. "Bring him on up," she said.

Ben traveled him to the window and watched.

Fid stuck his head in to get the corn, naturally.

Rachel said, "Pet him, Tee."

The girl's eyes brightened, Ben noticed, and she reached over to rub his nose, and between his ears. Ben jumped off and put his back up against Fid's rump to hold him there.

"What's she doin', Mama?"

"She knows it's an animal."

"She sayin' anything?"

"No."

In a minute, Fid pulled his head back out and Ben rapped him on a flank. The pony took off for the marshes.

"It's encouragin'," Rachel said, pulling the window down.

What was encouraging? For someone to pet a pony? Ben shook his head.

His mother was making soap from lye, ashes and grease that day and he was of no further help. So he went to Chicky. He gladly stayed until the boats came in and the catch was unloaded. It was shipped to Elizabeth City on a big sharpie.

Sunday was rainy but it was falling softly. Rachel got dressed in a dotted swiss and felt hat to go up to Mrs. Farrow's and read Bible with the other women from around Chicky. The nearest church was in Hatteras village and it was just too far to go unless there was a revival meeting. Then everyone went.

Ben knew he'd have to be alone with Teetoncey for three or four hours, but that was better than sitting in Mrs. Farrow's and listening to round-robin Bible; singing, "Jesus, Lover of My Soul." Those women didn't have a pump organ, but sang anyway. Mrs. Farrow used a tuning fork to get the right starting key. The men slapped their sides about that.

After his mother left on the sand cart, wearing an oilskin and sou'wester over the felt hat because of the dampness, Ben roamed around the house for almost a half hour, then decided to try to talk to Tee again. There wasn't anything else to do.

He went into the bedroom and sat down on the bed. She was sitting on the opposite side, staring out of the window; watching the rain.

She turned when he said, "I'll tell you some things."

She looked back at him, almost without blinking, as he began to talk about things that he knew. Whales or white porpoise or laughing gulls or eating-sized turtles. He told her that deer scratched themselves on the bark of old trees during tick season and that you could always tell when a raccoon had gone up a berry tree by the claw marks. He discovered that the worst thing in the world to talk about was fish. You catch and eat them and there is nothing else to say.

Then he ran dry and sighed, "C'mon."

He took her by the wrist into his mother's bedroom and showed her the pictures on the dresser. "That's John O'Neal and my brother, Guthrie."

She looked at them but the blank expression didn't change.

He took her to the opposite wall to show her the gold Medal of Honor, with its crossed oars. "Government gave that to my papa. He was a hero, Teetoncey."

Nothing.

Ben said, "Whew."

He led her back into the living room and sat her down on the couch. She folded her hands.

Then he thought about that British professor who'd come out to investigate all the words that didn't sound so strange to the Bankers at all. If the words were from Devon, maybe she'd know them.

77

He pulled a chair up. "If someone tells you they caught a slew of feesh, that's many. *Slew* is many."

"Mama is *couthy*. That means she's capable."

He pointed out the window. "That timber out there for the laundry line is a *postie*. An' we get *waspies* an' *nesties* in our chimney summers."

"*Disremember* is to forget an' *disencourage* means what it says. *Mindable* is payin' attention an' *studiments* is lessons . . ."

"We *traveled* him to you means we brought him to you . . ."

"*Swayzed* means it moved aroun' . . ."

"Fid an' Boo Dog are *critters* . . . I'm a *youngun'* . . ."

"*Fleech* means to flatter . . ."

Off-hand, he couldn't think of any more that the professor had gotten so all-fired excited about, but it didn't make any difference. He might as well have been talking to a postie.

She was looking down at the floor.

Ben said angrily, "Tee, why don't you get some sleep," and took her back into the bedroom. He thought he might have been better off going to Mrs. Farrow's and listening to Ecclesiastes.

He couldn't understand it. His mother seemed to have no trouble at all. She jabbered on as if she was getting answers to everything. And he'd never seen her so happy, not even when Reuben came home safe. He made a guess that after taking care of four men she was inspired to do all sorts of things, from making more dresses for Tee to getting Mr. Burrus to order some hair curling irons from Elizabeth City.

The clock ticked on and Ben slowly went out of his mind waiting for his mother to return.

10.

The next day Frank Scarborough and Kilbie Oden, who were twelve and thirteen, respectively, came by just to take a look. They stuck their heads in the door and got their look, but didn't say anything.

Ben watched Tee. She was on the couch. She didn't seem to know what to make of it.

Rachel said, "Come on in, boys."

Frank answered, "No, mam, Mis' O'Neal."

Ben was sure they did not want to be around a freak.

They pulled their heads back out. Frank was nice looking but Kilbie had bad skin. His mother daubed salve that contained sweet spirit of niter, and something else, on it. He was speckled white a lot of the time. But Kilbie was plagued with an unfortunate face, anyway. It looked like piecrust with a round nose jammed in the middle. His hair was reddish. But Ben had always said, "They're as good-a-boys as any."

Of the three of them, Kilbie, despite his looks, was the smartest, in Ben's opinion; including himself. He knew a lot about many things but he had his weaknesses, too. They had only "gotten" to Kilbie on one occasion, in Ben's memory, and it was over snakes.

It was around the time that Jabez Tillett took the three of them up the feeder ditch to Lake Mattamuskeet. Vines hung over that wine-colored ditch and snakes lay up in the vines. It was not a recommended trip for those who were skitterish.

That morning a few dropped into the boat and Jabez, Frank and Ben were frantic with the oars trying to get them out. They hit each other as much as they did the snakes.

But Kilbie stayed calm and wisely just reached down to pick them up one by one and toss them over the side. They weren't "pizen," he said. He even laughed when Frank hit Ben in the mouth with an oar blade, drawing blood.

Two days later they got back at Kilbie. They made a cut in the rear wall of the Oden's outhouse and found a long, crooked stick. When Kilbie came out just past sunrise and sat down Ben guided the stick through the hole and up. He aimed perfectly. Just as he jabbed it, Frank hollered, "Snake!"

Kilbie came out of the door as if his tail was torched. He ran across the flats with his pants down around his ankles. They heard his yelling in Chicky, and Mrs. Oden inspected his bottom for an hour trying to find fang marks.

But it did prove to Ben and Frank that Kilbie wasn't always smart, and that under certain circumstances he *was* afraid of snakes.

Kilbie seemed to be involved in everything around the village. He, and his older brother, Everett, were the ones who dressed up on the eve of January 6, old Christmas, in a cow's hide and head, to charge up and down the streets of Chicky, pretending to be Old Buck, which the British professor had said was a direct descendant of St. George's dragon. Actually, Old Buck was a direct descendant of the wild bull of Trent Woods, which was really an ox, according to Kilbie.

Ben went on down to the dock with Frank and Kilbie. High water had messed it up several times. It swayed some. John O'Neal had built it two years before he capsized. Filene and Jabez had worked on it twice, and Reuben had put in six new pilings on a trip home. Only time it was used for a boat was when someone brought a sharpie or bugeye along it Sundays to visit Rachel. The boys crabbed off it summers to pass time. They didn't eat the crabs. They were the same as "trash fish." Sharks, skates and the like.

However, Ben, Frank and Kilbie had also used the dock as a place to get away from prying ears. They'd been learning how to cuss the last summer and had spent some afternoons on the dock just cussing at each other between netting crabs. They had gone beyond "damn" and "hell."

Soon as they sat down, Frank asked, "You see her naked?" He was dying to know.

"Every pore of her," Ben answered proudly.

"How's she built?"

"All bones."

"Nothin' else? You know what I mean," Frank said.

"She's the same as Lucy, Frank," Ben replied, not really knowing, of course.

But he had seen Lucy in the pure ivory hull. They'd all three stood on a box looking into Lucy's room after she'd had a bath until Mrs. Scarborough came storming around the side of the house and threw a rake at them.

Kilbie said, "I can't figure out why she's speechless. It's the talk of Chicky."

"It's a medical word," Ben said. "She had her brains addled."

"Then she's crazy."

"I wouldn't put it past her."

Kilbie said, "Remember that mate, Armitage McNamara, off the *Sally Hubbard*? He come in on a surf. Prochorus Midgett had to rope him to get him off the island. I saw him. He was trussed up like a wild pig."

"We're not worried about that, Kilbie. She hasn't the strength to lift a bobbin."

"But I can't figure out why she can't talk. Even crazy people talk. Look at Mis' Peele. That's all she does. Not a word makes sense but they come out to never stop."

Frank said slyly, "Mebbe she don't want to talk? You thought about that?"

Ben hadn't at all.

84

Frank went on. "Mebbe she's an orphan an' lookin' for a good home."

Ben had to laugh. "Well, she could find a damn sight better than this one."

"Not if you're starved. You said she was all bones."

That was a thought. Although there weren't any on the Banks, there were orphans all over Carolina looking for homes.

Kilbie said, "Mebbe she's deef an' dumb?"

That was also a thought. Doc Meekins hadn't mentioned that. They talked on for about an hour until Frank had to go home. His papa docked about four usually and Frank had to help unload fish. Kilbie's papa was on duty at Little Kinnakeet station and did not fish in the winter.

In the house, Ben said, "Kilbie thinks she may be deef an' dumb."

Rachel answered, "Kilbie's taken up medicine now?"

11.

In another few days, Tee was almost recovered except that she was still speechless and acted like a spirit around the house. She sat a lot and stared with blue owl eyes. Ben could have sworn she found something remarkable in the corners of the living room. She'd seem to look vacantly into them for hours.

She was also having bad dreams. Ben was now sleeping in his mother's room which wasn't too pleasant at best. Rachel sometimes snored with a sound that resembled a file being drawn through an empty gourd. Then every night or so Tee would awaken them by screaming. They'd rush in and she'd be sitting up in bed, shivering. It would take a spell to get her quieted down.

By this time, Ben had decided she was definitely hopeless and began to wish that the British consul would take her off their hands. He did not mention that to his mother, though.

But aside from the bad dreams, she was well enough to do some things. Rachel had her helping in the kitchen although she wasn't of much use. She could dry dishes but she dried them as if she was in a dream. Her hands moved. That was about all. But Ben thought she was fattening up a bit though she ate no more than a thrush.

It snowed lightly on Tuesday, while they were parching coffee beans. Snow was a seldom thing on the Banks and it never lasted too long. The Gulf Stream winds and the sun melted it. But Tee watched it for several hours. The flakes were big and feathery.

Ben asked, "You think it snows in England?"

Rachel replied, "I would think so."

"It's a wonder it doesn't remind her."

"Mebbe it does."

Maybe eels could walk, too, Ben thought.

On Thursday, Rachel said, "Ben, I want you to take her out. Go somewhere with her. Get her out into the fresh air. I'll bundle her up."

"Go where?"

"Anywhere. Jus' don't take her near Heron Shoal or talk about the *Malta Empress.*"

That was a jest, Ben thought. He could talked about the devil and she wouldn't have known. He argued but ended up hitching Fid to the sand cart and helped her in. She seemed to go docilely wherever he led her. No different than Boo Dog, he thought.

There was a board seat on the cart and then a canvas bag beneath it, behind Fid's tail, to drop feet

in. It was mostly there for his mother, Ben assumed. Women were so finicky about their shoes.

With Boo Dog trotting on ahead, Ben got the pony going and headed for the beach. He thought he'd show her some wrecks and whatever else was around. Dead whale or bottle-nosed dolphin washed up. Maybe go on to Hatteras and show her the lighthouse. She'd never get a better view of shoals, with water crossing like herring-bones, than up those steps.

Had it been a stormy day she could see waves fighting each other on the shoals. They'd crash together and throw spray fifty feet up. It was the tallest lighthouse in America. Two hundred seven feet high. Ben climbed it when there wasn't anything better to do.

He began to get a good feeling even though he was sitting by a mummy. It was the first time he'd ever done this. First time to squire a girl out this way. "Goin' gallin'." Except usually the gal had something to say, he would think.

The sand cart rode smoothly, almost silently. The rims were wide on the two big wheels and unless the sand was deep and dry the tackie had no problem. And Fid was hardly overworked. Rachel used him to go to Chicky for groceries or on Sundays. Ben forgot about him most of the time.

They cut across toward the sea over the low dunes and clumps of juniper roots that had tumbled in on storm tides and were now half-covered. The gold dog was running out in front; Fid's mane was bouncing and quivering in the breeze, shaggy coat ruffling. It didn't take much to stir the sand and start it blowing about an inch off the surface. It streamed out behind them.

Ben glanced over at Teetoncey. She seemed to be coming alive a little. Her pale cheeks were turning red; her hair was whipping. The sharp nose was pointed into the wind. The large blue eyes were beginning to look around.

They broke to the beach at about the *Hettie Carmichael* wreck. She'd been a three-masted schooner out of Baltimore, grounded in the winter of '96. Keel long broken, and up on the sand, she was rotting out. The mast and rigging had been cut off. She was good for firewood now.

Ben said, "Shipwreck, Tee."

The eyes narrowed.

There were parts and pieces of wrecks, anything from bow or stern sections to ribbing, every few miles up and down the beach; some half buried in sand. Some surfacing again after a storm. Once they were stripped down, no one paid much attention to them.

Ben stopped and got Tee down off the cart, walked her over to the *Carmichael*'s stern and then persuaded her on up. The sun was out and the sea was behaving itself. It was a pretty day.

Ben thought maybe that just seeing a wreck would jog her memory and clear her mind. It didn't.

Mainlanders usually frog-jumped all over the wrecks. Tee just stood there like a statue; looking more at the beach.

Ben felt compelled to say something. "Spring an' summer, we sea-feesh all up an' down here. Haul nets. For croaker, spot, butterfish, sea bass, blues . . ."

For all she cared, Ben thought, they could be fishing for mule dung.

He got her down and back up on the cart. Now, he knew what it was like to be a nurse. He cut inland to circle around Heron Shoal and then dropped back down to the beach.

As they jogged along, Ben thought that if she'd been a boy and could talk and listen, he could tell her about Reuben's trip down Cape Lookout way to watch the whaling. Lookout was at the bottom of Core Banks, last of the real barrier islands, on south of Ocracoke and Portsmouth Island.

Reuben had sailed down as a boy, by himself, taking three days to go down and back. There were five or six crews camped from Shackleford Banks north to Hatteras in the spring, putting lookout "crow's nests" on the highest dunes and then waiting for the whales. They went out in boats and harpooned them; towed them ashore and cut the blubber out, boiling it in big kettles on the beach to get the oil. That went at thirty-five or forty cents a gallon. They'd also sell the whalebone "baleen." They got more than a dollar a pound for it, Reuben had once said. Diamond City, on Shackleford Banks, was the whaling capital of North Carolina.

Although there wasn't as much whaling now, Ben planned to take the same trip in *Me and the John O'Neal* when he could. But there wasn't any use in trying to tell her about it. She wouldn't be interested, anyway, he thought. British girls would be concerned with fairy tales, likely.

Going on south, he couldn't resist saying, "Ghosts out here at night, you know. They walk the beach in full moon." She was looking over the side, paying no attention.

One night he'd come out with Frank Scarborough and they'd seen something near the *Calderon*, which was a Spanish wreck. Even the shapes of the hulks were spooky at night. With silver light on them, they looked like wooden skeletons.

If the weather was good, it was a custom to take anybody from the mainland down on a full moon. Summers, especially. Once, they took Kilbie Oden's cousin, who was visiting from Charlotte, down to see them. He almost rendered his heart from fright.

Ben had put on a sheet and hid in the *Hettie Carmichael*. After Frank and Kilbie brought the cousin, Ben began making "wooing" sounds all over the place and then jumped up. What a story that boy had to take back to Charlotte, Ben often thought. But he admitted later that even he didn't like waiting all alone on the wreck until the others got there.

"What moon were you born under?"

No answer.

"Mine was dark. That means I'll never be thrifty an' strange things will happen to me."

No answer.

Why even talk?

But it was true. The moon controlled the tide, which everyone knew, and the tide controlled the Banks. Wood cut on a dark moon never burned well. No one ever planted a garden on a dark moon, and death always came on an ebb tide.

Ben got restless and decided to walk for a while. He got Tee down and turned her loose. She did seem to be interested in what was on the beach. She squatted to examine a Scotch Bonnet shell, turned a horseshoe crab over with her foot; then picked up a clam shell. She seemed to be looking at the lines in the shell.

Well, Ben thought, if that's what she wanted he could show her a pile of oyster housings ten feet high.

The reins had dropped off the seat and Fid was stepping all over them. Ben stopped long enough to take care of that, and when he looked up Tee was staring at him as if she'd never seen him before.

"Whew," he said. Maybe she was a ghost that hadn't died properly.

He sighed, "C'mon, Tee."

12.

He took her next to the store at Kinnakeet to show her off as much as anything. There were four old men sitting around the stove, as usual, spitting into the sandbox. All they ever did was talk wrecks, fishing and politics. Zion Fulcher was one of them. He had the stump of his leg up on a nail keg. They all looked over.

Ben said, "This is the British survivor."

Tee was almost hiding behind him. He stepped away.

"Name's Teetoncey. Temporarily."

Zion cackled and spit a brown bullet of dark plug into the sandbox without losing a drop. "Heerd so. Looks it, all right. I'm proud to know ye. You swum in, eh? Had a rough toime?"

Ben explained, "She can't talk."

Zion said, "Well, oi can." He said direct to Tee, "Women an' younguns don't fare well in wrecks. Lost a lot of 'em off the *Home* down by Ocracoke."

Ben thought to himself: Zion, why are you bringing that up? That was Racer's Storm, in 1837, before you were even born.

Another old man, toothless as a scallop, said, "I feeshed plenty some that year."

He hadn't even heard what Zion said. Ben sighed. "Tee, let's go." He took her hand.

Zion spoke again. "Ben, Mis' Creedy come up to say that heifer got out o' powsture. Got her earmark on it. Split to right. You see it, you tell Mis' Creedy."

"I will, Mr. Fulcher."

Zion spit again, a good eight feet, and perfect.

"You tried shootin' a gun off up near her nose? Ears moight be clogged."

Ben shook his head. They hadn't tried that. It was an idea, though.

They went on toward Hatteras Light, which had a stripe like a candy cane around it. Ben wanted her to see Diamond Shoals and the whale-oil beacon lamps. They were about the best sights on the island.

To the west was Buxton Woods. A strange place, in Ben's opinion. It was only twelve or thirteen miles from the Gulf Stream. Lemons grew there. Chicky could be freezing while people sat around in Buxton in shirt sleeves. There were cottonmouth snakes there, and one man had sworn he'd seen an alligator at one pond between the ridges. Everyone thought he'd lied, though no one said so.

Ben got Tee going up the steps of the lighthouse. The ladder well was dim and Ben liked to shout in it because it echoed. "Two hundred sixty-eight steps to the top, Tee," he yelled.

"Tee . . . Tee . . . Tee."

The echo funneled up and out.

She was ahead of him. Climbing silently.

"Mebbe we'll see a school o' feesh . . ."

It echoed nicely up the tube. "Feesh . . . feesh
. . . feesh."

At about ninety steps, Ben stopped to holler
again. There, the sound seemed to go down and hit
the bottom, then slither back up the clammy bricks
to glide out into the Hatteras graveyard sky. Step
110 was better, but 90 was all right. Ben cupped his
hands around his mouth:

>Kill a cat
>Gut a bat
>Last one up's a
>Bloody rat

Ben waited. Down it went. Then up it came.

>BLOODYRAT
>Bloodyrat
>bloodyrat

Ben grinned and looked up to see how she liked it.
She was kneeling down and shaking. He peered
closer. She looked peaked, too. Ben sighed. "All
right, let's go back down."

So they went down and had pork sandwiches at

the base of the light, Ben not even trying to talk; then they headed on north, Boo Dog riding the cart, too.

Tee kept looking out to sea and without thinking Ben trotted the tackie right up to Heron Shoal. Suddenly, he saw that Teetoncey was staring out to the white water where it crossed the bar, probably to the very spot where the *Malta Empress* had crunched in. She had panic on her face, and her mouth was quivering. Ben wondered if she'd begun to remember.

Quickly turning Fid up the dune, he cut across straight home.

As soon as they got inside, he said, "I think she may remember somethin'. She started gettin' panicky at Heron Shoal."

"You didn't, Ben . . ."

"I forgot."

Rachel groaned and then took Tee into the bedroom to show her the new gingham dress she'd finished while they were gone. But Tee just threw herself across the bed.

A few minutes later, Rachel got Ben aside. "Where else did you take that girl today?"

"I showed her the *Carmichael*, took her to the store at Kinnakeet, an' got her partway up the lighthouse steps."

"Lord above," Rachel said angrily, "you've got no more sense o' feelin' than your papa had."

That always made Ben fume. "Don't say anything about him."

"I'll say he was about as tender as dried oak, and you're the same. Makin' her walk those steps; takin' her by Heron Shoal."

Ben went out, slamming the door, feeling a rage. He hadn't meant to upset the girl.

13.

Tee had a bad dream after midnight. The screams ripped the quiet and they rushed into the room. Ben stood sleepily in the doorway while his mother calmed her down.

Then Rachel turned. "Ben, go back to sleep. She's wet the bed. I'll change her an' settle her on the couch."

Ben shook his head in disgust. Someone that age wetting the bed. Worse, it was his own bed. He returned into his mother's room and slipped under the covers. He could hear his mother talking softly to the girl and pulled the pillow over his head, sighing deeply.

The morning broke cold and windy but clear. Tufts of frost around the grass clumps in the yard began to melt as the sun mounted.

Ben hardly looked at Teetoncey. There was no reason in the world why she couldn't get up and go to the outhouse like everyone else. He got dressed and hauled in the day's supply of wood.

After breakfast, while Tee was sitting by the stove in her nightgown, staring at the red embers lying inside the bottom vent, stroking Boo Dog's head absentmindedly, Rachel said, "Ben, haul that mattress outside an' throw it over the sawhorses to air."

That was the everlasting end. Ben looked over at Tee. "Why can't she do it? She wet it."

Rachel whirled around, white lines spreading away from her lips. "I'll do it, Ben," she said savagely. "I don't need your help. Why don't you jus' get outta here. Go anywhere you'd like. Jus' stay away."

Ben stared at her a moment, a sudden flare of anger and resentment rising in him. If that's the way she wanted it, fine. He strode past Tee to get his heavy coat, boots and bob-cap.

At the door, he said, "C'mon, Boo."

The big dog angled his eyes up without even raising his head from between his paws. They said, Don't be silly. The girl was still rubbing along his back.

"Boo!"

The dog ignored him and closed his eyes again.

Ben slammed the door and went into the yard. He stopped, shaking with rage, wondering what to do. He couldn't see the tackie around and had no particular desire to ride him anyway. He thought about going back in and getting Reuben's gun to shoot some ducks. But that didn't appeal to him, either.

Finally, he went mumbling north to the Odens.

Kilbie was out by the side of the house, splitting wood. The first thing he said was, "Saw you out with that girl yestiddy. You in love with her?"

Ben laughed. "How can you be in love with a vegetable? That's what Doc Meekins called her. That's what she is. I'd just as soon love a carrot."

"I saw you two cuttin' across toward the beach on the cart. You looked high 'n' mighty."

"You know what she did last night, Kilbie?"

Kilbie shook his head. He had the pimple salve on.

"Wet the bed. My bed. Whew."

"You're foolin'."

"I wish I was."

"Why don't you get rid of her?"

Ben laughed sourly. "I ain't the one's in love with her. Mama is."

Kilbie said, "Somebody'll come from England an' fetch her back, sooner or later."

"Sooner the better. You wanna go for a sail?"

Kilbie looked out across the sound. "That's a mean wind, Ben." Whitecaps were spread all the way to the mainland.

"It's dyin'."

Kilbie looked north. "I don't think so. There's an eyebrow on those low clouds." They had begun to blossom within the last hour.

"She'll come down to a whisper by noon."

Kilbie shook his head.

The more Ben thought about it, the more it appealed to him. Out there, away from the house, away from his mother and Teetoncey, he could clear the cobwebs from his head. He could think about going on up to Norfolk and finding a ship. Reuben had

102

gotten a berth just by asking around at the chandlers.

"See you bye 'n' bye," said Ben, and walked south again, swinging well out to the middle of the island to avoid his house. He spotted Fid munching down in the marsh but kept going until he reached the thicket where *Me and the John O'Neal* was hidden.

He inspected the seams. There'd been enough rain the last two months to keep it somewhat damp. The thicket branches shaded it from the sun so it hadn't dried out too much. Besides, he'd done a careful caulking job in September.

Turning the boat over, he pulled the sails from under the thwarts and shook them out; then dragged the boat down to water's edge. He looked out across the sound. The whitecaps were chopping-up but the breeze seemed steady. He liked it that way. The best sails he'd had was when the water was cresting white; when the wind would pocket and heel the boat over, driving it to let a stream of bubbles boil in the wake.

A few times he'd shouted for the wind to blow harder, feeling the spray off the gunwales in his face; yelling as *Me and the John O'Neal* bounced across the sound, bow pounding and strumming as it hit the short-spanned waves.

He stepped the mast and rigged the jib, then snapped on the mainsail. It wasn't rigged exactly like the larger Creef boats. Ben had made his own design. But it cruised along, proved steady and handled nicely.

Ben pushed her on into the water, jumped aboard, and then poled away from shore with an oar. The water was shallow for three or four hundred feet. There was a lee at the thicket, the land curving in. He drifted for a hundred yards while he pulled the jib up, and tied it off. It flapped harmlessly. Quickly, he hauled the main up; grabbed the sheet rope and then jumped back for the tiller as the wind caught the sail. The boat began to drive forward and Ben yelled with joy as it shot out of the lee.

It scudded into the whitecaps, heeling over sharply, and Ben moved the sand ballast bag with his foot, knowing instantly he could just as well do without the jib. There was more than enough wind for the main, and he felt a slight ticking in his stomach. But he couldn't go forward to lower it. She'd come around and flip over if he let go the tiller.

So he decided to run before the wind and wait until it slackened off. He had the sheet rope, which controlled the mainsail, in his right hand and steered with his left.

Me and the John O'Neal flashed south down the wide Pamlico and Ben settled back, not even minding the cold spray that stabbed his face, hanging in the air a few seconds from the overtaking wind.

He had in mind running down to about opposite Buxton Woods, then tacking back, hugging the east shore if the wind was still setting to south. He'd let the boat run free, keeping just inside the channel where the surface wasn't quite as rough as on the shallows. It would be an all-day trip.

Everytime he was out he realized more and more what his papa and Guthrie had found on the water. It was an escape from all the harassments of land. There was no one to say what to do and how to do it. Just the keening of the wind and the swish of the prow.

Ben had not looked astern for a long time and did not know that the earlier eyebrow of storm clouds had advanced until the sun suddenly vanished. He turned and saw them. They were rolling down on the Banks in a fat, gray fold; full of wind.

He studied them and the ticking came again into his stomach. He looked off to port and saw the Kinnakeets. He hauled up a bit on the sheet rope and laid pressure on the tiller, beginning to angle toward shore. He could dock over there and walk on home; come back in a day or two when the wind was back to its prevail. He figured he was about five miles offshore.

The first gusts of the approaching storm slashed across the sound a few minutes later and Ben felt his heart begin to pound. Then a gust hit like a giant fist. He could not let her to the wind quick enough, nor let the sheet rope fly in time. *Me and the John O'Neal,* carrying too much canvas, flipped over, throwing Ben into the icy water. His breath was snatched away as he went under.

He came up beneath the sail, which had spread out on the chop, pushing it up with his head; gasping; feeling as if his lungs were on fire.

He stayed still a second and then felt his way

along the mast up to the boat. It was on its side. Grasping the gunwale, he kicked around it and then pulled himself half out of the water, clinging to the overturned hull.

Panting, already feeling he was starting to freeze, he knew he couldn't right; bail her out. Summer, he could have. But his hands were already going numb. The wind felt like a knife on his back and shoulders. He kicked his boots loose to let them fill and sink. Now, the sharp cold of the water was numbing his feet.

He could only think, *This is what happened to Guthrie.* He knew he could not hold on much longer.

Twenty minutes later, Hardie Miller, of Kinnakeet, running before the wind to get to dock and safety, spotted the overturned boat and hauled around in his big Creefer, its sails wisely reefed.

He came up smartly to the *Me and the John O'Neal,* saw Ben clinging to the skag, and yelled, "What the hell you doin' out this mornin'?"

While his two crewmen handled the Creefer, Hardie threw a stiff line over Ben's head. It hit cruelly. "Hang on to it," Hardie yelled, and Ben felt himself being yanked away from the hull.

There were hands under his armpits suddenly and then he felt himself flopping to the floor boards like a mullet. He lay there gasping; numbed.

"Git on into that shelter," Miller ordered harshly, having no use for boat stupidity. Ben crawled forward, almost automatically.

On his hands and knees, pooling water, he began shaking; he could hear his own teeth clattering. Then Hardie stooped in and tossed a blanket to him. "You have to be crazy, Ben O'Neal," he said.

Ben didn't answer back. He couldn't.

A half hour later, with the righted *Me and the John O'Neal* towing behind, the Creefer docked at Kinnakeet.

Ben was still shaking, as much from fright as from cold when Hardie Miller ducked back in and yelled, "Now, git your lil' ass on up to that store an' dry off. Then why don't you take an ax an' chop that boat up 'til you learn how to sail."

Ben nodded and crawled weakly out of the shelter cabin; then rattled and shook all the way up the dock. He heard Hardie Miller shout after him. "You git my blanket back soon's it's dry."

Some of the same old men were sitting around the stove when he came in. One cackled. "You go for a swim today, Ben?"

Ben closed his ears and stood by the stove, shivering.

Mrs. Gillikin came out from behind the counter. She said, "Ben, strip your clothes on off. I'll hang 'em to dry."

He felt humiliated. Nothing had gone right since that castaway girl come up out of the sea.

At about two o'clock, Kilbie Oden rode up to the O'Neal house and knocked on the door. Rachel answered.

"Mis' O'Neal, Ben turned over in the sound. But he's all right. Hardie Miller got him out. I tol' him this mornin' that wind was too mean."

"Where is he now?"

"Kinnakeet store. Dryin' off. Prochorus called Filene an' I saw Jabez out on the trail a while back. Jabez said to tell you that Ben's all right."

For a moment, Rachel felt vast relief, a weakness over her whole body; then it turned to blazing anger as Kilbie rode away.

14.

The squall passed over the Banks, mostly gusts of twenty to thirty knots, and a few bursts of rain. It cleared again by late afternoon and just before sundown, Ben turned up the lane and walked toward the house. He'd borrowed shoes in Kinnakeet to make the walk home. He didn't relish entering. It was certain that some loose mouth had told his mother. That's all anyone ever did out there. Gossip.

He took a breath and went on in.

Rachel came out of the kitchen. He didn't really know what to expect. He saw Tee sitting on his bed looking at one of the Chicago catalogues.

"I hope you got your good taste today," his mother said. "I see you lost your boots."

Yep, she knew.

"I'll tell you one thing, Ben O'Neal. I want you to bring that boat to our dock an' keep it there. You're gonna start mindin' me."

He was about to say, "What boat?"

"I've known you've had one for months. Least you could do is be honest."

Ben reddened.

"What happened?"

"Gust hit me. I was carryin' too much canvas." That was the truth. Next time he'd know better.

Rachel shook her head, wanting to be gentle with him yet feeling he must be made to understand that water was a killer. She sighed. "Anybody but a pure fool wouldn't have taken a small boat today 'less they had to."

"I got picked up."

Rachel nodded. "By the grace o' God." Then she said tiredly, "Ben, I'm plenty full o' death and destruction. Now, you don't know how to sail an' until you learn, I want that boat tied up where I can see it. You may think you're John O'Neal, but you're not."

Rachel started back for the kitchen, wishing that Reuben was around to talk good sense about wind and water.

Ben said after her, sullenly, "I wish Papa was alive."

Rachel stopped, anger welling back. "So do I. Maybe he'd tell you he'd learned his lesson. The hard way."

"He'd of taken a boat out today."

Rachel's eyes hardened. The boy had to know sometime. She'd thought about telling him long before but the right opportunity had never come up. More than that, she had not wanted to destroy his hero worship. Better it be destroyed, though, than have Ben six fathoms under.

"Let's go in the kitchen, so that child won't hear us. No use gettin' her upset, too."

Ben followed her in, bracing himself. He stood by the sink. He just wanted to get it over, whatever it would be. He felt exhausted.

"Now, I want to tell you somethin' that no Keeper or surfman here will tell you about your papa. They've got their special honor. All they want to talk about is heroes. Never the fools."

Ben's mouth dropped. Was she calling John O'Neal a fool?

"Your papa just as well as murdered those two men he took with him to his grave."

"That whole crew was volunteer," Ben blurted frantically. "Jabez tol' me."

"Did he tell you the surf was twenty feet high that night? That every man in the crew told your papa it was sure death to go out? Did he tell you that they all had a lil' will-makin' ceremony before they went out, led by your papa?"

Rachel's eyes had tears forming. She would allow only a few. Her voice stayed steady. "Ben, he knew he wasn't goin' to come back. It was only lucky that four men got ashore after he capsized. Steerin' oar in his fists, he was tellin' the sea he was stronger than it was. Now, isn't that a fool?" There, she had it off her chest.

Ben fled out into the night and went down to the dock. He clung to a piling head, feeling sick. But he refused to cry.

About seven, Ben made his way up the ladder

into the lookout cupola of Heron Head station. He'd
been told that Keeper Midgett was up there.

Filene sometimes liked to have a pipe in the lookout after supper. He'd watch the lights of passing
ships; look south to the warm beam of Hatteras
Light; north to the faint wand from Bodie Island
Light.

In the darkness, Ben said, "Cap'n Midgett, can I
talk to you a minute?"

There was something in the boy's voice that was
queer. Subdued. Hurt. Filene recognized it. He
struck a sulphur match. In the flare he saw that Ben
looked like a horse had back-legged him in the breast
bone.

"Yes, Ben."

Mark Jennette was also up there, studying a ship
with the long glass. He said, "Howdy, Ben."

Ben nodded.

"Cap'n, is it true John O'Neal was a fool the night
he capsized?"

Filene peered at Ben in the darkness. "Who tol'
you that?"

"Mama."

Filene said, "Ben, I heerd you dumped that lil'
sailboat today. You ought not to be out under a
squall sky. Your mama's upset."

Ben pressed again. "Was he a fool, Cap'n Midgett?"

Filene looked out to sea for a while. "Ben, the surf
was twenty feet high that night. I frankly don't
think your papa had too much hopes o' gettin' back."

"Then he was a fool."

Filene answered slowly. "Depends on how you look at it, an' who looks at it. I will say one thing. There was a ship out there in distress. People pleadin' to be saved. Now, do you think he could 'ave turned his back on 'em?"

Ben stood for a moment, nodded, then said, "Thank you, Cap'n."

He wound on down the ladder.

Filene said to Mark Jennette thoughtfully, "He may have the makin's, at that. He could be as rough as John when he's growed."

At home, Ben faced his mother once more. He said, "John O'Neal couldn't have turned his back on those people."

Rachel felt herself cracking like glass; coming apart inside. In all the years, she had never thought of that one simple thing. She'd only thought of how senseless it was to row out to death. Not why. Now Ben had told her.

She reached out for him and pulled him tight against her so that he could not see her tears. Then she said, softly, "No, son, your papa could never do that."

Ben sighed deeply.

15.

At calm daybreak, when he awakened, Ben felt better than he had for a long time. A cloud seemed to have lifted from the O'Neal house. Perhaps the last two days had been a storm, with fair weather following.

He hitched Fid to the cart and then went north to pick up Kilbie and Frank. He realized now how close he'd come to death out in the Pamlico. There wasn't much doubt that if Hardie Miller hadn't happened along, he would have slipped on under. Next time, he thought, he'd reckon respectfully with squall clouds.

They rode along to Kinnakeet, Frank and Kilbie asking all sorts of questions about the boat tipping over. Then they brought it back home overland, strapped to the cart. Ben put it down by the dock but didn't launch it.

Rachel came out and took one look at the name on the transom. She laughed. "I might have known it."

Frank and Kilbie went back to Chicky while Ben

and his mother returned to the house together, walking close.

In the afternoon, Ben said, "I'll take Tee somewhere if you want." He felt he owed his mother a family favor.

"That would be nice," she replied.

Rachel got Tee dressed, putting the new red bobcap Mr. Burrus had sent over on her head.

Ben hitched Fid up again and they went north in the cart up to Pea Island. He thought Tee might like to see the snow geese. They fed on the salt-marsh cord grass over by sound side.

On the way, he tried to talk to her once more, but it wasn't easy. The only thing he could think of was to tell her about John White, Virginia Dare and the lost colony of Roanoke Island. They were headed in that general direction.

Tee watched the countryside while he talked and Ben finally lapsed into silence, too, knowing that her visit, if anyone wanted to call it that, couldn't go on forever. Any hour now, they expected the British consul to get a message to them saying they knew who she was; then she'd leave.

Meanwhile, Ben had made up his mind to make the best of it; help when he could. Try not to let those blue owl eyes make him uncomfortable; be patient with her.

The trail turned inland and the flats unrolled, not too far below Oregon Inlet. As usual, there were thousands of snow geese there. Doing what Ben had seen them do for years. Feeding, flapping, fighting;

making noises at each other. The whole marshy flat turned white come the first frost.

He stopped the cart, keeping Boo Dog tied in it. The dog loved to barrel right into the thick of them, sending them skyward. It was fun when it happened. But not this day. The girl might not appreciate it, anyway.

He noticed that she was watching the geese intently. Her eyes lost the dullness and seemed to sharpen. They went back and forth and there was a funny expression on her face when a vee of them came winging in and lit.

Ben wondered if she really knew they were geese. There were also some whistling swans and gadwalls out there. Perhaps it was only his imagination, but she seemed excited.

When the ganders bulled their way around, squawking and fluttering a few feet, tail feathers rigid, Tee sat forward.

A bald eagle floated and spiraled along overhead for a moment, wheeling to take a look at all the commotion below.

"Bald eagle, Tee," he said.

He thought he saw her eyes lift. Then realized he'd also pointed. She'd caught the motion of his finger.

They stayed for almost an hour, Ben watching Tee more than the birdlife; beginning to think that perhaps something was left in her head; that she wasn't totally crazy. He kept watching her on the way home.

About a mile away from the snow geese flats, he untied Boo Dog and let him jump to earth. The dog began running out ahead, as usual. Sniffing at the bushes; stopping to lift a leg; then rocketing out again.

Tee had turned her attention to Boo Dog, and Ben watched, too. It suddenly occurred to him that he'd never really looked at Boo very much. The muscles were rippling under his gold coat; his tail was arched up. The wind picked at the shag on his back, blowing it like a grain field.

Tee didn't take her eyes off Boo until he finally disappeared into the brush to the west.

Then she began watching the tackie.

Ben thought, All right, what do you see there?

Fid was holding his head high. The wind was blowing his mane. The heavy muscles were gliding on his rump and hind quarters.

Ben was so intent on watching Tee that he hardly realized a small hand had come over and was resting on his. He glanced down at it and then across to her.

Her eyes were still on Fid. He didn't think she knew she'd done it. He tried to hold the reins very still, wondering what was happening.

He was waiting for her to look over and smile; even say something.

But then a skinny rabbit scooted across the trail ahead and her eyes went to that. The hand dropped away.

At home, Ben said, "She touched me, Mama. Comin' back."

"She did?"

"I don't even think she knew it."

Rachel looked over at the girl. "Ben, I swear Doc is wrong. She's not a vegetable. Everday I see a sign of somethin'."

16.

The next morning Ben rode south to Mis' Creedy's on the edge of Buxton Woods.

Mis' Creedy was one of the foremost people on the Banks. She had been a schoolteacher and had then come into some money when her father died. The main reason she'd moved to the Banks was to paint birds, and those they had ample of. Ben thought she did a good job with herons and snow geese. But her grebes and egrets didn't look alive, somehow.

She lived in a cottage, one of the finest on the barrier islands, on the sound side, midst myrtle and live oak and clematis. Made of juniper, pine, cypress and some mahogany salvaged from a ship, it had a brick fireplace with great iron firedogs from the north. She'd bought it from Cap'n Tillett's family after the widower passed on at ninety-three. She was not Banks-born but people had taken to her. She did not even look like a mainlander. She was chunky and had a ruddy face. The women forgave her for wearing men's pants because she had to slop around in the marshes so much to paint the birds.

Ben said, "Mis' Creedy, you got any books on London I could borrow?" He knew she'd traveled over there.

Surprised, Mis' Creedy answered, "Why, I have a few books on London, Ben." He'd borrowed books before but they'd always been about the sea. "Why London?"

Ben lied. "I'm jus' curious. I saw a ship yestiddy with London on the stern." Ben crossed his fingers. If she'd think for two minutes, she'd know a ship never got in that close unless it wrecked.

"Do you want one with pictures?"

"I don't know."

Mis' Creedy walked over to bend down by her bookcase. "I think the best thing I have here is a Baedeker."

"What's a Baedeker?"

She pulled out a small book that was bound in red leather. It wasn't much bigger than two hand palms. "It's a travel guide, Ben. I used it all over London. It's crammed with information. It even has maps in it."

"Can I borrow it?"

"Why, I'd be pleased to have you read it," said Mis' Creedy. "It certainly won't hurt you."

"I appreciate it."

"Take this one, too. *The People of London.*"

Ben took them and even tried to read some of the red-covered book going home but Fid kept bouncing him. It did say on the front page: "London and its Environs (whatever that meant); Handbook for Travellers by Karl Baedeker; with 4 maps and 24 plans; Leipzig: Karl Baedeker, Publisher."

Ben did not know such books existed.

He decided not to tell his mother about the books he'd borrowed. She'd mention it to someone, and then they'd mention it to someone else. Then somebody would figure out the purpose, having nothing better to do. Sooner or later, Kilbie would come up to say, "You sure you not in love with that vegetable?"

He hid the black-covered book in his bottom drawer and then took the Baedeker down to the dock and began to scan it. In a few minutes, he almost dropped it into the water. On page 26, under the heading of *Shops* was "Durrant's, 116 New Bond Street." Same as the label on Tee's dress.

Ben was stunned.

He ran back into the house and found the salt-stained shoe. Back on the dock, he moistened his finger to bring the printing in sharper. He made out, "Hook, Knowles & Co., 65 Bond Street." He found that shop on page 29.

Then he made a guess as to where she might have bought other things: *Gloves at Wheelers; underclothing at Sweats & Wells, on Oxford Street; hats at Mrs. Heath's on St. George's Place . . .*

It seemed there wasn't any general store, like Burrus', with everything under one roof.

He figured out where Tee might have bought candy. The place was Fuller's, at 28 St. Swithin's

Lane. He even picked out a restaurant where she might have gone with her parents. Simpson's, the ladies room upstairs.

Ben read on in amazement.

London had almost five million people and that was more than North Carolina, South Carolina and Virginia put together. Or so he thought. It had subways and electric railways and tunnels under the River Thames. It had omnibusses (with garden seats on the roof) drawn by three horses. It had 500 newspapers and 500 music halls and one place with a French name where there were wax statues of everybody. It had eighteen big railroad stations and maybe a thousand small ones.

There was a fish market named Billingsgate that was big enough to put Bodie Island in; the Metropolitan Cattle Market had 10,000 head of beef, 30,000 sheep and 1,000 pigs, all on the hoof, and the best time to go there was Monday before Christmas. Everybody bought their vegetables and flowers at a place called Covent Garden, and the best time to go there was Easter Eve. Leadenhall Market had chickens and game on the claw. Ben reminded himself to tell Mr. Burrus about that because he was trying to raise prize White Leghorns.

It was some fine place in which Teetoncey had lived, Ben finally concluded.

Before he left the dock, he picked out an area for her house. Baedeker's told him that the finest places in London proper were in Chelsea and around Belgrave Square. He chose the latter because it sounded so fancy when it said, "Belgravia consists of handsome streets." He then selected Eaton Square as hers.

He felt the fool, but he was enjoying it. Now, he'd give her a name. He wanted it to sound elegant and looked in Baedeker's at the section on private mansions. There was the Apsley House, the Dorchester House; the Lady Brassey Museum. Then he saw the Lansdowne House.

He looked at it a long time. But that could well be her name, he thought. It certainly could. *Elizabeth Lansdowne.* She sure wouldn't be called Willy Ann or Lucy.

Ben laughed to himself because he'd never done anything so idiotic in all his days. Then he went on up to the house.

Tee was on the couch.

He said, "Elizabeth Lansdowne? Do you hear me? That your name?"

He did not get an answer, but for the first time it didn't bother him.

In the kitchen, he said, "You know they got tunnels under the River Thames in London?"

Rachel was peeling potatoes. "No, I didn't know that." She wondered where he'd heard about it.

17.

Ben worked for Mr. Burrus early in the day. As he went about sweeping out, dusting the shelves and splitting kindling, he kept thinking about the Baedeker book, imagining Teetoncey going to the Metropolitan Cattle Market on the Monday before Christmas or to Covent Garden Easter Eve; riding the electric railway or seeing that place where everyone was in wax statues.

Having never been to any town larger than Manteo, the Dare county seat, which was huge in comparison to even Hatteras village, it almost seemed impossible that London existed. Reuben had told him about Norfolk, Baltimore and New York. But they now seemed small alongside London, if the red-covered book spoke the truth. He couldn't wait to get back home to read the other one.

After the noon meal, he emptied the ashes in both the kitchen and living room stoves, filled the wood boxes; then got the books out and was about to head for the dock when Rachel said, "Take Tee with you.

It's warm enough." The sun was out, and the temperature was in the mid-fifties.

Ben shrugged. It didn't matter. While he read, she could sit and do what she usually did. Stare.

Rachel noticed the books under his arm but paid no attention to them. Ben was often reading something. She said, "Don't let her fall in."

Ben nodded, took Tee in tow, and went out.

He showed her the small shad boat which was off to the side of the pier, on the shore. She simply looked at it.

"That's the mainland over there." He pointed.

Her eyes went in that direction.

He got her settled on the dock, legs dangling over, and then sat down beside her, putting his back against a piling header. He glanced at the Baedeker and had an idea. He unfolded the railway map of England which was in the front of the book. "Remember this?"

He stuck it under her nose and watched her eyes. They went away from the map and began to concentrate on the minnows that were swimming around the pilings. Ben sighed and put the Baedeker away to read *The People of London.*

They did some incredible things. They could walk by Buckingham Palace and see the queen now and then. At the end of the third chapter, it said that some people went to France on "holiday."

Ben closed the book and looked out across the sound. There was enough breeze to kick up whitecaps. The water was the color of coffee with a lot of milk in it. It was clear enough to see Long Shoal Point which was on the mainland well above Wysocking Bay. A schooner was beating down the channel and some Creef boats were out.

France wasn't much further away than the mainland if you lived in London.

Ben shook his head and glanced at Tee. To think that speechless thing had probably gone to France.

Why, it took them a day's sailing just to get up to Shallowbag Bay in Manteo where the only foreigner was a half-Greek who ran the cafe.

Ben read until almost sundown and then took Tee back up to the house.

Rachel asked, "How'd she do?"

Unable to contain his exasperation, Ben answered, "She watched the gudgeons."

Sometime during the night he had a dream. As dreams go, it faded in and out and didn't make much sense. But it did involve Elizabeth Lansdowne and a fourteen-room house, along with Queen Victoria, Buckingham Palace and Birdcage Walk. Also, some talk about going on a holiday in France.

Just as it ended, Ben said, "You know, you're pretty."

Teetoncey laughed back impudently, "You fleech me, Ben O'Neal."

He awakened and lay very still for a while, looking out at the stars, thinking about it. Most of it had come from those books. It was all crazy, as she was.

But she seemed to be getting to him. Like as not, he thought, she'd stay a mystery until the British consul came to get her.

Ben rolled over on his side in an attempt to go back to sleep.

Rachel stirred.

18.

Ben rode over to deliver a pint of *penetrate* to Mrs. Scarborough. Lucy was sick. When he got back, Rachel asked, unconcernedly, "Where's Tee?"

"She's here, I guess," Ben replied.

"I thought she was with you."

Ben shook his head.

Rachel said, "Oh, Ben," and they both ran out into the yard. She wasn't in sight, nor was Boo Dog. They began shouting her name but Rachel finally said, "That's not gonna do any good. I'll go up the trail an' you look along the shore."

"Boo has to be with her," Ben said. He followed her around like a lamb now. So he began yelling for Boo, walking north along the sound.

Ben went almost a mile, searching for footprints in the sandy mud; calling for Boo. There was no trace of her. He began to worry, though she couldn't very well get off the island without a boat, and there wasn't anything to hurt her. No animals large enough; the cottonmouths were sleeping the winter out.

Then he thought of the sink sand patch just below Salvo. All she'd have to do is step into it, and fare the' well without a gurgle. He and Kilbie had tossed rocks into that sink patch; they'd gone down in five seconds. It had swallowed a sheep whole.

Heart in his mouth, he broke into a run and burst through the thicket looking for tracks. Boo's or hers. But the mud near the sink patch hadn't been disturbed aside from some heron marks. She hadn't been there.

Ben yelled for the dog in vain, and then began running south.

In the distance, he could hear his mother hollering. "Teetoncey! Teetoncey!" It carried on the wind.

He ran past the house to find Fid. He could cover more ground on the sand pony. Then, out of the corner of his eye he caught a splash of red down on the dock.

There she was, sprawled out on her stomach, looking down at the minnows; Boo Dog draped out by her side, stupidly asleep.

Ben blew out an angry breath and walked down. He shouted at her. "Why didn't you answer us, you idiot!"

She lifted her head and gazed back at him innocently.

Boo also lifted his head. That made Ben wild. He kicked Boo in the stern and said, "Least you could have done is barked."

Then he pulled Tee roughly to her feet. "C'mon."

He waited in front of the house until his mother

got back. She was puffing coming up the lane. "Where was she? My heart's poundin'."

"Out on the dock."

Rachel said, "Teetoncey, child, don't go out of the house unless you tell me." Instantly, Rachel thought— Now, that's a silly statement.

The girl gazed blankly at Rachel as she had at Ben.

"You see," Ben said.

Rachel nodded. "I guess we're gonna need to watch her closer now."

Ben mumbled, "Or put a bell aroun' her neck."

Rachel said, "She didn't mean to," and they went on in. Suddenly, Rachel stopped. "Ben, you realize she put on her own coat an' hat? That's another good sign."

Ben snorted. "If she'd gotten into that sink near Salvo, that's all that would have been left of her. That hat floatin' on top."

It happened again Sunday.

Rachel went to Mrs. Burrus' to read Bible, and Ben stayed around the house to keep Tee company but finally in late morning decided to put *Me and the John O'Neal* back in the water. He wanted to check the rigging, too. Hardie Miller had been none too easy-handed when he'd righted the boat.

Ben saw that Tee was safely on the couch, still in her nightgown, turning the pages of the Sears catalogue slowly. That was enough to occupy her for an hour, at least. He went down to the dock and began work on the boat.

About noon, Rachel returned and saw the night-gown on the floor in Ben's room. She hurried outside.

"Tee down here anywhere?" she asked.

Ben straightened up with a start. "She's in the house."

"No, Ben. Where's the dog?"

"He went off early." Every so often, Boo would prowl away on an expedition, sometimes going as far as Hatteras village.

"Well, she's gone again," Rachel said, with a slight annoyance in her voice. "I'll change my shoes . . ."

My fault this time, Ben thought, and went to find Fid. But that sand sink hovered in his mind. Carrying the bridle and bit, he hurried along the shore until he located the pony. The tackie wasn't too far away, engaged in his usual gnawing. Ben quickly slipped the bridle on, mounted him, and went at a gallop for the sink, leaning over along the way in hopes of seeing her tracks.

He crashed through the thicket and pulled Fid up short, hopping off. No footprints were visible. He mounted again.

Which way now? That girl was getting to be too much for them he thought.

He cut across island and headed for Heron station, thinking she might have walked the trail; maybe someone spotted her.

Luther Gaskins was out behind the station, sunning himself after noon chow and reading a month-old copy of the Norfolk *Pilot*.

"You see Teetoncey?" Ben shouted.

"Nope. Haven't seen her since we got her outta the surf."

"She's lost, Luther. She did it Friday, too. She's startin' to roam worse 'n' heifer."

Gaskins got up. "You check the sink near Salvo?"

"She's not there."

"I'll tell Cap'n Midgett. How long's she been gone?"

"No more'n an hour."

Gaskins went into the station, and Ben slapped Fid's behind, rode down over the sand banks and headed south along the beach, thinking she might have gone back to the *Hettie Carmichael*.

He looked far ahead, on past the *Hettie*, but there wasn't a soul on the beach. Seldom was, on winter Sundays. Boo Dog had certainly picked a terrible time to go hunting, he thought, pounding along on Fid. If worst came to worst, he'd run Boo down and have him track her.

He drew up at the *Carmichael* and looked around the wreck but she wasn't there. He checked the sand around the stem. The tide was ebbing out and there weren't any shoe marks.

Ben didn't know where to go next. He thought of riding on down to Kinnakeet station, but that was a good four miles, and she couldn't have very well covered that much distance.

Jabez Tillett loped up on one of the big mules. "You spot 'er, Ben?"

"Not a hair."

"Well, you go on inland. I'll ride this way. Cap'n Midgett called Pea Island an' New Inlet. We'll find her."

Ben rode on up over the bank. Even though he knew the barrier islands were the safest places in the world if there wasn't a gale, he started to worry the way he'd worried Friday. And this time, he'd been responsible.

He rode south for a quarter mile, saw his mother on the trail, and pulled up.

"Any sign of her?" Rachel asked dejectedly.

Ben shook his head. "Filene has turned out search crews from Pea and New Inlet, too. They're on the beach now."

Rachel said, "Ben, think hard. Where could she have gone? I even looked in the closets."

"She's jus' wanderin', Mama."

"Think of all the places you've taken her."

"She couldn't get as far as Hattrus now."

"Closer places."

"I checked the *Hettie Carmichael*."

Then Ben thought about the snow geese. "Mebbe she's up inland on Pea Island."

"Go, Ben," Rachel said.

Ben cracked Fid's ribs with his feet and headed north.

In twenty minutes, he was on the flats and saw a small figure ahead, barely a speck. He muttered, "Damn me, there she is."

He rode on up, and there she was, watching the

geese. They squawked and scattered as he got closer and Teetoncey finally turned to look at him.

He felt that same mixture of anger and relief that he'd felt on Friday, but there wasn't any use to yell at her. Ben said, "Girl, we're gonna put a rope on you," and slid off the pony.

He stood over her. "You know what you've caused? Whole Lifesavin' Service is out lookin' for you. Mama is walkin' the trail . . ."

Tee just stared up.

Ben shook his head. He reached down and pulled her up, then said tiredly, "Throw a leg over that pony."

She stayed motionless.

He repeated it.

Finally, he picked her up and struggled her aboard Fid. He waited for her to take a hold on him. She just sat there. He turned slightly. "Tee, put your arms around my belly." That didn't work, either. So he reached back and took her hands, clasping them around his middle.

"Let's go, Fid," he muttered, and slapped a flank.

They trotted toward Heron Head station.

Filene was in the yard. He said, unexcitedly, "You found 'er, eh?"

"She was watchin' the geese."

"That's a good thing to do on Sunday," Filene said calmly, giving her a long look. "She's pert today, ain't she? Got some color in her cheeks."

Then he casually walked inside to phone the other stations and call off the search. Ben thought it was impossible to know what would excite Filene and what wouldn't.

He trotted Fid on home.

Not much was said the rest of the day but that night, after supper, Rachel began to talk. Before she opened her mouth, Ben believed he knew what the subject would be.

"I thought about it all afternoon. She may be gettin' too much for us, Ben. She ain't ours. An' if somethin' happened to her out here, I'd never forgive myself. If she fell off the dock or got into that sink sand . . . I think it would finish me . . ."

Ben nodded. He could understand that, after what had happened to his papa and Guthrie.

"I do see signs o' improvement, but they might be jus' wishful thinkin'. An' we may even be hurtin' her in some way. Mebbe a doctor could unlock her mind . . ."

Rachel moistened her lips and continued, hating what she was thinking and what she had to say. "The other thing, Ben, is that ever' single day, whether we know it or not, we're gettin' more attached to her. Even if she's started to do pesky things . . ."

That was also true, Ben thought.

"So, much as I hate to do it, I'm goin' to talk to Filene tomorrow, have him call Mr. Timmons an' the British man an' tell them to come an' get Teetoncey. It's best, Ben."

He looked over at Tee. She was studying the red embers in the bottom stove port. *Elizabeth Lans-*

*downe, or whoever she was, would finally be headed
somewhere soon.*

He hadn't thought it would end like this, nor had
he thought it would matter much, one way or another, when she did have to go. But suddenly, it
did. He couldn't bring himself to say that the girl
should be sent away. And he figured his mother
would be the last one to do it.

He frowned. "Mebbe we should wait. Someone'll
claim her."

"It's been almost a month now. I know it takes a
long time for letters to get to England an' back but
we mighten know for three months. Worst o' the
winter hasn't hit . . . she could get sick. At least, in
Norfolk, they could take proper care of her. Not that
I'm not tryin'."

Ben finally nodded. Yes, it was probably best.

He got up, tugged on his coat, and went outside.
The Banks were bathed in moonlight, and he began
crossing toward the beach, trying to think how his
father might handle this. Like as not, he'd take it in
stride, consider her a speechless critter and go about
doing what had to be done.

By the time Ben got back from the beach walk
he'd made up his mind to brace himself and take it
the way any surfman would. Had the castaway girl
had some senses, it might be different.

Mid-morning of the next day, Ben hitched Fid to
the cart and then watched his mother drive off
toward Heron station. She was wearing a black shawl
on her head to keep her ears from smarting.

He went back into the house and said to Tee, "You'll be better off." Steel was the way to handle it.

Since it was Monday, at Heron station they were drilling with the beach apparatus and Filene was busy but Rachel called him up from the sands. The wind was brisk, cold, and the flag was flapping; the wave tops were white out to sea.

"Turned into a nice day, hasn't it, Filene?" Rachel greeted him.

He squinted at her. "So will tomorrow."

"I do think it's warmer this winter than last."

Filene kept squinting at her. The only time she ever came near a surf station was to borrow the doctor book or have a Keeper make a call on the phone. "Might be."

"Well, we haven't had a good freeze yet."

"Not yet." Filene scanned down toward the beach and the men, then turned his blocky face back to Rachel. "You didn't ride up here to talk about freezes."

Rachel said, "Filene, I, uh, jus' wondered if you'd had any word from that British consul?"

"Not a word."

"I do deceive that it takes time, Filene, but I jus' wondered how long we might be havin' Teetoncey."

"She startin' to give you trouble?"

"Not a bit. She's good as gold. It's jus' that I didn't want Ben to get too attached to her."

"I see. You want me to call Mr. Timmons? Have him call the consul?"

Rachel swallowed and took a deep breath. "Not at all, Filene."

Filene nodded.

Pulling the shawl tighter around her head, Rachel said, "Well, I best go back home. Good day. I'll see you bye 'n' bye."

"You do that, Rachel," said Filene, as she walked back to the cart. He shook his head as she slapped the reins on Fid's back and turned him south.

In the living room, Rachel said to Ben, "I couldn't do it, Ben. I jus' couldn't turn my back on this girl."

It was certainly hard to know how to figure anything, Ben thought. Elders could never make up their minds.

19.

Crisis passed, the O'Neal house settled down again and for the next week they kept a sharp eye on Teetoncey. But she didn't attempt to roam far. Once, she headed for the dock to watch the minnows and Ben quickly fell in behind her. He took her to the Burrus store twice and she sat quietly by the roaring stove, chin in her hands, as he worked.

Nothing much had changed. She was still having those nightmares and still silent as a mountain stone. There were moments when Ben felt sorry for her and equal moments when he wanted to kick her in the flanks and make her talk.

Then, for a day toward the end of the week, the sky was mackeraled, gathering rolls of nimbus clouds by nightfall. Finally, the nor'easter set in during early morning hours, predictable by the barometer in the living room. The needle fell like a shot duck.

By noon, there was a forty-knot wind howling over the Banks, driving cold rain ahead of it; peppering the windows. It gusted now and then, shaking the silvered house.

As could be expected, soon as the weather hit, Rachel went into her usual gloom. Tee was even worse. She couldn't light anywhere for long, Ben noticed. She kept going to the windows; listening and looking.

Working on a bufflehead decoy he'd roughed out of pine in October, he wondered again about Reuben. He was due up the coast about now from Trinidad, the Barbadoes, and wherever else he'd gone. For all Ben knew, he was off the Banks this very afternoon, reefed-up and ploughing through; taking water over the decks.

He glanced at Tee again. She was now sitting in the straight chair, drumskin tight, staring at the door. The storm plainly worried her, he could see. She'd probably never been in a house that danced because of a gale. Well, it did.

He kept on carving.

What always bothered him most about being indoors during a blow was the terrible quiet, aside from the clock going *tick-tock* endlessly; the moan of the wind under the doors and windows.

He purposely knocked the decoy off the edge of the table. It hit the floor with a bang.

Tee let out a gasp and jumped up.

Rachel looked at her a moment and then said, "I'll put some yeopon on."

Tee sat back down.

Ben noticed her hands were trembling now and his mother saw it, too. Whenever there'd be a big gust, she'd tense up like an edgy quail.

145

Most of the long afternoon was torturous and Ben knew his mother was turning something over in her mind. She'd keep looking at Tee out of the corners of her eyes, talking occasionally to her about things that didn't matter; had nothing to do with the weather. She also kept looking at the clock.

Ben was puzzled and could feel something in the air. His mother was back at her habit of chewing her lip; scratching alongside her jaw; weighing thoughts mentally. Then she read the Bible for a while.

At about five, storm still hammering the Banks, Rachel rose up and went into the kitchen, calling for Ben to follow. She seemed calm and organized, as *couthy* as she'd ever been.

Standing by the stove, she said quietly, "Ben, we're gonna try somethin'."

"What?"

"Try to unlodge whatever's in her mind. You see how she's acted all day?" His mother nodded toward the front room. "So skitterish. She's never been this way before. Only when the gale hit."

"She's jus' scared of it," Ben replied.

"Mebbe that's what it's all about, Ben," his mother said. "Mebbe what happened to her in that other gale put her mind in prison. It's worth a try."

"What is?"

"Takin' her back to Heron Shoal. Let her see it all over again."

Ben was shocked. This wasn't anything to do with *penetrates*.

"I know," Rachel said, reading his face. "But I've thought it all out."

"It'll jus' scare her worse, Mama." He swallowed. "It may even kill her."

"Or cure her, Ben. Now, you get dressed, an' I'll bundle Tee up."

Ben hesitated.

Rachel said confidently, "Lord above, I'm no doctor, but we've taken care o' ourselves out here for two hundred years without one, an' most of the time we've been right. Jus' usin' common sense an' whatever herbs there is aroun' us . . ."

"But, Mama . . ."

"I'll take the blame for whatever happens. If she's a vegetable, as Doc says, then it can't hurt her. If she's not, we'll jus' see. Now, take her to the beach."

It did not make much "common sense" to Ben. All that was out there was breakers and cold rain; wind that would bend you double. But he went into the bedroom to get his oilskin.

He listened as his mother helped Tee get dressed. She was saying, gently but firmly, "You should see for yourself what's down there, Tee. Then mebbe you won't be frightened anymore. You'll get cold an' wet, but we can dry you off."

Ben went out to the living room.

Tee's eyes were wide. On her face was the same near-panic of that second night when she'd tried to talk but found that she couldn't. Ben watched as his

147

mother tightened the clasps on one of his old rain-coats and then put her own sou'wester on Tee's head.

Rachel said soothingly, "You jus' hang on to Ben. Now, go, the both of you."

At the door, Rachel said to Ben, "You cut acrost straight to Heron Shoal. No other place. You jus' let her take a good long look an' then come back."

As he was closing the door, she added, with determination, "Ben, if you got to drag her, get her there. Make her look."

Outside, the rain was like icy birdshot, fired by the lancing wind.

At the end of the lane, when they passed the last live oak, Ben stopped to look at the girl. The small face was powder white. He took a firmer grip on her hand, not at all certain his mother was doing the right thing.

She held back. Even in the darkness, her eyes seemed as big as grommets.

"You're goin'," Ben yelled, and pulled her along.

They doubled over, bucking into the gale. After a few hundred yards, she fell but Ben got her back on her feet again. Already, they were soaked.

Three-quarters of the way there, she fell again over a piece of driftwood and started to cry. By this time, Ben could feel the sand shuddering from the surf slam; hear the water roaring.

He shouted, "It's not far now, Tee."

Suddenly, her free hand flashed out desperately, glancing off his chin, as she struggled to get away.

Surprised, Ben almost lost her but then took another hold on her wrist and pushed on, half-dragging her. Once, he turned and saw that her eyelids were locked shut. He handled her with the only thing he thought he knew: strength.

Finally, he got her over the last rise and a few feet down the slope, almost to the foamy white water. The roar of the surf was deafening. It was every bit as high as the night the *Malta Empress* grounded. The breakers hit like cannon volleys.

Out there, somewhere, was Heron Shoal, wild and churning; sending spray thirty to forty feet into the air.

Ben held her by the surf's edge, water washing around their feet, and shouted into her ear, "Look, Teetoncey. Look, I tell you."

She finally raised her head and opened her eyes, staring out toward the shoal. He saw terror come into them, and then her face knotted as a scream knifed out. He'd never heard anything like it.

He looked toward Heron and almost saw what he thought she was seeing as she relived it—the bare-masted ship, heeling over, crashing on the bar; her mother slamming against the deck housing and tumbling forward in debris; the icy curl of sea that had lifted her off the deck; her father towing her; then the breakers. At last, peaceful darkness and no memory.

The scream knifed out again and again, unlodging that wild night from her mind; releasing her from her own prison.

She lunged suddenly, breaking away from Ben, plunging out into the wash. Then she screamed hysterically, "Mother . . . Father . . ."

For a few seconds, Ben was stunned; almost paralyzed but then plunged after her, grabbing at her shoulders before she reached the breaker line. She twisted away with a strength he didn't think possible, and he grabbed again, finally locking his arms around her waist as a surge of sea caught their legs, sweeping them in.

Still clinging to her, sputtering, Ben managed to rise to his feet when they grounded and struggled her through the foam at the tide line. He yelled at her angrily, "Dammit, you do that again an' I'll bust you one . . ." Then he was sorry.

Her head snapped around and up, water streaming over her face. Even in the dimness, he could see that her wide eyes were filled with horror and fright. And the way she was looking he was sure she didn't recognize him. Ben felt helpless.

Teetoncey looked back at the sea again and then her whole body began to shudder in sobs. Ben thought he heard, "My father . . . my mother . . ."

He turned her around and started back, an arm tight over her shoulders; gale still buffeting their backs. She sobbed all the way home.

Rachel met them at the door and took Teetoncey into her arms.

Ben started to say something, but Rachel shook her head and led the girl into the bedroom.

Almost an hour passed.

Ben did not really want to go into the room and his mother had turned the knob behind them, anyway. But the sobbing had stopped and for almost twenty minutes he'd heard two different voices in there.

Boo Dog was sitting outside the door, his head cocking over one way, and the next, as he, too, heard the different voice.

Ben moved around restlessly, feeling strange. For reasons he could not quite understand, he was suddenly weary. It had been but a short walk to the beach and back, but he felt completely exhausted; as tired as when he'd been fished out of the Pamlico. His head seemed drained out, too. It was hard to think or know what to think.

Then Rachel opened the door. There was a soft satisfied smile on the bony face. She said, "Everthin's gonna be all right, I think, Ben. She don't really remember us, as yet. Things are still cloudy with her. Mebbe the Doc can explain it. But jus' act natural. Come on in . . ."

Ben moved slowly, almost with dread.

Tee was on his mother's bed, sitting up, a blanket around her shoulders; a pillow at her back. Her face was pale and worn; eyes puffy again like they were the first night, reddened, but open this time. Her hair was a little mussed up, wet around the edges.

Ben noticed that she wasn't smiling. Just looking curiously. Her eyes dropped to Boo Dog a moment and then came up.

Rachel said, "Ben, this is Wendy Lynn Appleton, of London, England."

Ben nodded shyly, not certain how to react.

Rachel went on as if she was making an introduction up at the Burrus store. "This is Ben, of course, who found you, along with this ol' hound."

The girl nodded back just as shyly, then said politely, in a very British voice, "I want to thank you, Ben . . . for all you've done."

She could make sense. She wasn't a vegetable.

Then Ben felt himself doing a fool thing right there in front of her. Tears were coming down his cheeks even though he didn't want them to.

Keeping a taut line on her own emotions, maintaining a calm that had been passed along through two hundred years of Banks' women, Rachel nodded a pleased affirmation. Ben wasn't made of solid oak.

Though she vaguely remembered this boy with the dark, curly hair, the castaway girl was puzzled. Why should *he* be crying this night?

Soon, she would know the whole story of what had happened to young Ben O'Neal since she'd arrived, so unexpectedly, on the Outer Banks of North Carolina.

ABOUT THE AUTHOR

Theodore Taylor was born in North Carolina and began writing at the age of thirteen as a cub reporter for the Portsmouth, Virginia, *Evening Star*. Leaving home at seventeen to join the Washington *Daily News* as a copy boy, he worked his way toward New York City and became an NBC network sportswriter at the age of nineteen. Since then, he has been, variously, a prize-fighter manager, merchant seaman, naval officer, magazine writer, movie publicist and production assistant and documentary filmmaker. He has written six books for adults and seven for children, including *The Maldonado Miracle* and *The Cay* which won ten literary awards, among them the Lewis Carroll Shelf Award and the Jane Addams Peace and Freedom Foundation Award. Mr. Taylor and his wife and three children live in Laguna Beach, California.

ABOUT THE ILLUSTRATOR

Richard Cuffari's main interest in life is "making pictures." Since his graduation from Pratt Institute in Brooklyn, he has illustrated over eighty books—garnering along the way accolades from the Society of Illustrators, the American Institute of Graphic Arts, the Children's Book Council Showcase Exhibit, the Christopher Award, and several others. Born in Brooklyn, New York, Mr. Cuffari still makes his home there with his wife, Phyllis, their four children, a dog and four cats.